A Strand of Truth

Cinzi Lavin

A Strand of Truth is a work of fiction. Names, characters, events and incidents are the products of the author's imagination. Any resemblance to actual persons, living or dead, or actual events is purely coincidental.

A Strand of Truth. Copyright © 2023 by Cinzi Lavin. All rights reserved. *No part of this book may be used or reproduced in any manner whatsoever without the express written permission of the publisher, except for the use of brief quotations in a book review.*

Cover art: Adobe Stock Image

ISBN: 978-1-7366350-2-5

For R.L.B.

PART ONE

CHAPTER 1

You hear a lot of stories in my business. Everyone wants to talk. Psychologists say people only open their mouths to speak if they need something, and if that's so, then a lot of people need to have their stories heard. At least it seems that way to me.

It wasn't always like this. When I first started out, I couldn't get people to say a word. But then again, I was using a spotlight and intimidation tactics, but I can't really talk about that. It was a government investigative position, let's just put it that way. I happen to come from a powerful family, and some well-placed relatives grudgingly put my name up for an opening. I say "grudgingly" because I didn't fit the bill of the usual type of guy who gets that sort of job. I'm a bit, well, *flamboyant*, at least around the edges. But everyone there at the bureau got along with me well enough; I'm punctual, personable, and impeccably dressed, but most importantly, I'm intelligent. And in that line of work, it pays to be very, very smart. Nobody could deny me that. They might've had a few uncharitable names to call me behind my back, but I had a string of academic credentials that were pretty hard to top. That and a squeaky-clean record meant I never felt beholden, even if I did get some elite-family endorsements.

And so I worked there for a while but eventually, even I could tell the problem wasn't anybody else's unjustified homophobic discomfort or justified resentment at my inherited connections, but something about the structure of the job itself that just wasn't fitting my abilities. I'm no hard-boiled agent. Hell, half the time I would've rather done shadow puppets in those rooms to entertain the suspect instead of leading interrogations that invariably went nowhere.

Then one day, one of my boss' higher-ups called me in. I'll be honest: I felt pretty intimidated. Generally, my boss would've given me a heads-up for something like that, and he didn't, so I worried. However, he was very cordial and we chatted happily about this and that, so after a few minutes, I realized that whatever his objective was, it probably wasn't to fire me.

He reminded me of that old phrase, you know, the one about catching more flies with honey than vinegar. He said I wasn't very good at being the vinegary type—a point upon which I immediately agreed—and he told me they'd been trying to think of alternate ways of using me, particularly ones in which I could use my sunny side to its best advantage. I'll never forget the question he asked me next: *"Who do people willingly talk to?"*

I cast around in my thoughts. Becoming a priest was out. But as it so happened, that afternoon I'd gone for a haircut, and that's when it hit me: a hair stylist. Although I'm somewhat reserved, partly by nature and partly because of my line of work, even I felt comfortable talking openly about a lot of things with the guy who did my hair at the salon.

Of course, my answer turned out to be right. As the higher-up explained, the bureau had arranged for me to work undercover as a hair stylist. Sounds crazy, but it was actually a brilliant plan. It began with the necessary training, in which I was immediately enrolled. As I mentioned, I'm smart and I'm a fast learner. I managed the course in record time and even learned how to cut hair with a straight razor from an old Italian gentleman who was a master at it. So few people know how to do that these days; it was a valuable skill to acquire. Hairdressing wasn't exactly what I'd call my niche, but I enjoyed it, and everyone was happy to accept the openly gay guy. I had more female friends than you can imagine while I was at school.

So, with my new identity and my ivy-league credentials now officially replaced by the fabricated history of having had a few failed years at a mediocre community college, I was able to get work at an upscale unisex salon in a location in Chicago where I might come in contact with the type of people who might have the kind of information we wanted. It was up to me to get them talking. It was a lot easier than you'd think.

I quickly discovered that everyone trusts a hairdresser. Criminals couldn't wait to talk about their mad exploits, or discuss dreams of what they wanted to do with their ill-gotten gains. It was pathetically sloppy of them, I'll say that. I could've been . . . well, I *was*, and they found that out the hard way. Of course, they never knew it was me who informed on them, but just the same, I didn't feel any remorse for what I was doing. If these people were dumb enough to talk, they deserved what they got.

Our success rate skyrocketed, and suddenly everyone really seemed to appreciate me for the first time. Christ, talk about everyone loving a stereotype. Maybe that's just me being bitter that I couldn't be successful sitting behind a desk wearing a custom-made suit, but put a hairbrush in one hand and a can of hairspray in the other, and suddenly I'm the star of the team. Oh well; no use dwelling on such things.

The point is that the setup worked magnificently, and year by year, I got better and better at it. It was fun in a way, and pretty low-stress. I worked mostly with women who were jovial, and a few other gay men who were usually okay. Sometimes the women were a bit mentally unbalanced and occasionally the men were pompous, but overall, no worse than any other working environment, I'd have to say.

But it was the customers who fascinated me. I admit I started out being totally bored by working on anyone who wasn't a target. It meant hearing useless information; things I couldn't bring back to my superiors that wouldn't help solve any outstanding cases or prevent any crimes. For about a year, I felt that way, but then the stories started to click, if that makes any sense. Especially if it was a longtime customer, it became kind of like a soap-opera. I couldn't wait to hear the next installment the next time they came for a trim or to have their roots done.

It was sort of a side-bonus of the work, getting an intimate description of real-life stories as told by the participants (or witnesses, as the case may be; just as many people talk about their friends and relatives as they do about themselves).

There are so many tales, I wouldn't even know where to begin recounting them: lost loves, strange coincidences, heartwarming stories, and vicious acts that would make your blood run cold. And all of it all the more moving because it wasn't something an author or screenwriter had cooked up, but something completely real. It's true what they say about truth being stranger than fiction, believe me.

But then one day, something happened that set me on the path of the strangest and most astonishing thing that had ever occurred in my life. And if it's okay with you, as ironic as this may sound, I need to talk about it.

CHAPTER 2

I had this customer. He was about forty-five, fairly well-dressed, seemed like a bright guy, and he really didn't say much at first. I mean, he was congenial and all, but he didn't strike me as an extrovert. This is pretty typical with straight guys. They aren't quite sure how to take you—like if they're too friendly you'll assume it's a cue to start hitting on them, but if they're too quiet, they think you think they're in the closet or something, so they try to strike a balance by being distantly pleasant. A lot of plastic smiling, and all that.

But there's only so much you can say about the weather, and the more our dialogue developed over the months, the more he became at ease with me. It's amazing how you can read people after you've had a thousand strangers sitting in a chair underneath you. Frankly, I think I developed better interrogation skills in the beauty shop than I ever did working for the government. Not that I was ever blunt—you do it all subtly: "And how did that make you feel?" "Now is this your first wife or your second wife we're talking about?" "I imagine in that income bracket there isn't anything you can't afford," and so on.

The guy eventually told me he was a genealogist. He worked for some large organization and basically researched people's family trees. Sounded like a perfect job for an introvert. Also, oddly enough, he didn't seem to have any family of his own, so maybe researching about everyone else's relatives made him feel he was part of the great forest of human genealogy, lingering somewhere in an immense grove of other people's family trees. He was often quite a bit more well-versed about people's ancestors than they ever would be. A lot of times when he gave them information, they didn't care. They weren't really all that interested in their great-grandmother's brief stint as a European opera singer or their great-great-grandfather's twin brother who died at birth. (I could only imagine what he would've discovered if he ever got his hands on my real last name. Then again, when you come from a family like mine, you've been thoroughly briefed on who you are, going back at least ten generations. But still, his jaw would've dropped if he ever knew who was really cutting his hair. I'm an important person. Not so important that I have a Nando's Black Card, but then, those are almost impossible to get.)

But as he came to see me over time, I began to think of him as this vast repository of family memories. He was a storehouse of information. I grew to like him as a bland but forthright person and despite myself, I became slightly intrigued by some of the facts he occasionally shared with me. For instance, I found out that if siblings marry other siblings (such as Joe Jones and Jane Jones marrying Mark Martin and Marcia Martin), their relation to each other is both as sibling and sibling-in-law, which sounds wickedly incestuous but actually isn't. He even explained the second-cousins-twice-removed thing to me, but honestly, I still can't remember how it works. He said there are charts online I could always consult, so I'll rely on that if the time ever comes. And of course, I learned about all manner of stepfathers marrying stepdaughters after the mother died, and first cousins marrying each other, and all sorts of sordid little genealogical tales that only someone who has his face stuck in vital records registries eight hours a day would latch on to as something to lift the spirits a little. I suppose there's a certain twisted comfort in knowing that hundreds of years ago, people were just as naughty as they are today. Must be a great way to break up an endless stream of names and dates.

I hate to digress, but this is one of those stories that just came to mind, the kind of thing he'd often tell me, and it was one of the ones I found memorable. He said he was researching this English family's history and found the baptism record of the client's great-great-great-grandmother. Then years later, at the same parish church, was a record of her marriage. The witnesses were the groom's sister and the bride's brother, and their parents were in attendance. It was a June wedding. She was eighteen and he was nineteen. He also found land records indicating that they became the owners of a small rural farm featuring a modest house with a thatched roof, as well as cows, sheep, and chickens, according to tax records. He was happy to be able to report these details to the client. As he continued on in his research, he found the baptism of their first child, named for her maternal grandmother, which took place at the same parish a year later. He said it made him feel something for these people when he saw the most important events of their lives, recorded in ornamental handwriting in church records by dutiful priests with ink pens.

He was next anticipating to find the record of another such christening perhaps a year or so later, but instead discovered a town death record for the young wife. A case of pneumonia had carried her away, leaving her new husband and eight-month-old baby girl behind. He said he'd actually wept. Something about this family had so touched him that he was genuinely saddened by what he found. He checked to see if the man ever remarried, but apparently, he did not. He died in his early forties of unknown causes, having raised his daughter on his own and married her to the client's great-great-grandfather. Something about the sadness of the dissolution of that family lingered in his voice as he told me. I was unexpectedly moved, too. I never did forget that story. I asked how the client reacted when he told them this bit of family history, but he said they were just hoping for some sort of breakthrough proving they were descended from William the Conqueror, or some similar nonsense. He said he gets a lot of those. Everyone wants to be royalty.

But back to the main point, he'd come for haircuts regularly for about two and a half years when one day, only a week after his last cut, he surprised me by showing up without an appointment. He always made appointments—weeks in advance—but even odder, he wasn't even close to due for his next. Some particularly fastidious clients need a "placebo trim" between cuts, which they think will make a difference even though nobody in their right mind—not even a hairdresser—would ever notice, but you get used to accommodating people's eccentricities about their personal grooming. However, this guy wasn't one of those types. Not at all. He was completely predictable, which is why I couldn't fathom why he'd come. As I put the apron around him, he leaned slightly towards my ear.

"Please help me," he whispered.

My first reaction was that he was coming out and either wanted me to help him adjust or possibly deflower him, but that didn't really fit his character. He never mentioned a girlfriend, but I just knew he was straight. Probably too nerdy to attract women. Possibly asexual, even.

Just to be safe, I quietly said, "I'm sorry, but I don't date customers."

He said nothing but shook his head while staring intently at me. So I knew it had to be something else. I glanced around. Fortunately, my colleagues were taking their afternoon break down the street at the local coffee shop, one had gone home early with cramps, and the only other person in the salon was the receptionist at the desk, way down at the other end. I leaned over his face, pretending to comb and trim his sideburns.

"What's the matter?" I whispered.

"Can you hide me? Take me with you. I'm being followed," he hissed.

Somehow, in an instant, an internal shift took place and I was no longer the young, hip hairdresser with the listening ear. I was an agent again, and I was intensely aware that the man before me was genuinely in fear. He was too rational and too intelligent a man to react this way for no reason. I had to think fast. I stood back and appraised his look in the mirror.

"Hm, you'll have to give me a minute," I announced, feigning indecision. "I can't quite decide what to do with you today. Whichever way we go, I'll want to make sure it suits you perfectly. You know me. I don't like to get anything wrong."

He nodded and his face relaxed a little. He knew I understood and that I was going to help him.

I pretended to fuss with his hair as I considered all the options. Could he be someone sent to blow my cover? Highly unlikely. Nobody could create a secret agent *that* boring. Could he be in some kind of illegal trouble that I wouldn't want to get mixed up in? I seriously doubted it. He wasn't the type. What was the nature of the trouble pursuing him? A couple of neighborhood thugs? I glanced at him in the mirror. His eyes were shining with terror. No, this was big. Guns, car-chases, the works. Besides, he'd never have come to me if he were scared of some bruiser—he'd go straight to the police for that. This was something he *couldn't* take to them, something that demanded he seek help from someone who was, at best, only a marginal hope—his hairdresser. I concluded it must be very bad, indeed.

I worried about bringing him back to my place. I never like having people over, just in case I were ever attacked by someone who wanted to put me out of commission, because then they'd have to kill them, too, as a witness, but I guessed that level of danger might be a given in whatever we were about to face, so I decided bringing him home would be best until I could find out more. Also, I had to be careful not to reveal who I was. I had a pistol in the glove-compartment of my car, but a hairdresser whipping out a gun might seem a bit suspicious, so I hoped I wouldn't have to use it. The only catch would be getting him out the back door and into my car without being seen and without the receptionist becoming suspicious.

I pretended to lean in to cut a bit off the top.

"My car's parked out back; I can take you to my place. Just have to figure out how to get you out of here," I whispered. "Are they watching?" I asked.

"Yes," he whispered. "Outside the shop." He nodded toward the front window. I took a sidelong glance and noticed two men who'd been standing there since shortly after he came in. They looked professional. I wouldn't be able to guess who sent them until I knew more about what the situation involved.

Meanwhile, he began sweating bullets. He was terribly nervous. I forgot that as a professional, I was experienced in handling this kind of situation and he wasn't. I patted him on the shoulder.

"Don't look so worried. I promise not to cut your ears off," I quipped.

By that point, I had a plan in mind. I walked up to the receptionist's desk.

"Rosa," I told her, "I am having an absolutely splitting headache. I was up late last night drinking with some old friends from out of town and I just can't struggle through this day any more. Can you possibly reschedule my evening appointments?"

She agreed.

Then I added, "And forget about a charge for this one," indicating my client. "Just nervous about a big job interview and needed someone to talk to. You know," I shrugged, rolling my eyes.

Rosa nodded and looked over the appointment book while I glanced past her out the front window. I was pretty sure they were armed, but there were only two of them. I didn't want them getting too good a look at me, so I thanked Rosa and strode past the client into the back room, saying loudly over my shoulder that I had to get a particular product to use on him.

As soon as I was behind the curtain, I grabbed a pack of cigarettes that Lola, the owner, always left on the table. Nasty habit. She only smoked at work and didn't want her kids to know, so she left the cigarettes at the salon. I stepped out the back door into the fading sunshine and lit up. I don't smoke, but it was the perfect excuse to have a look-around. I unlocked my car after making sure nobody had been placed out back. Now I was able to tell that although they were professional, they were sloppy. Either that, or they had a guy hiding in the dumpster, which was doubtful.

I dropped the cigarette and twisted it under my shoe, going back inside to collect my client, bringing a bottle of finishing spray with me.

"Now *this* is good stuff," I explained, holding the bottle close to him so he could pretend to read the label. As he did so, I whispered "When she's distracted, go in the back room and wait for me." He nodded.

I removed his apron, then I said aloud, "Hang on. I think Darcy has some." I walked to the hairdressing station closest to the receptionist, opened the top drawer as if to get a styling tool, and proceeded to drop a large box of hairpins, which scattered everywhere at my feet.

"Oh, great!" I wailed.

Rosa looked up from her cellphone, on which she was texting, and dutifully said, "Here, let me help you."

"No," I told her. "It's okay. My mess, I'll clean it up." As I stooped down, I held my head and groaned a little to remind her I wasn't feeling well.

"Please, let me get it," she begged, walking around the reception desk and crouching to retrieve the pins. After ten years in the business, I'd come to rely on the fact that people are always predictable—they'll invariably help if they can.

In a flash, the genealogist disappeared behind the back curtain. I was still standing next to Rosa, who was bent over picking up pins, when I faced the front door and called out, "No problem. I didn't realize the time either. See you soon. And hey—good luck with that interview." Obviously, no one was there, but the vocal misdirection would make her think she'd heard my client taking his leave out the front. People are constantly extrapolating from tiny hints of information. We really only see a few clues and our minds fill in the blanks. I would have bet money that she'd swear under oath that she'd seen the client walk out through the front door. Her memory would adjust to the conclusion she'd drawn, rather than working from actual fact. It was a handy facet of human nature which could be exploited on occasions such as this.

"Are you sure you don't mind doing this?" I asked her.

"Are you kidding?" she replied, without looking up. "I'm almost done. Go home. You need to rest."

"You are simply the *best*," I told her, heading to the back of the salon. "Have a good night," I added, as I slipped behind the curtain.

My client, who was standing silently in the back, waited as I grabbed a couple of ratty old aprons that we use as extras or when we're doing a particularly messy color job. "Straight to the teal car," I said. "Passenger side's unlocked. Nobody's out there."

After opening the door, I took a quick look to confirm we were alone and then made a beeline for the car. My client got in and after I started the engine, I told him to slump down and concealed him beneath a pile of aprons.

I'd barely started to back out of my parking space when a bullet hit the passenger side of the car near the side-view mirror. It was a lucky miss for us, coming from what was probably close range. I had no intention of counting on any more such luck, though.

"Stay down," I ordered, spinning the wheel as I reversed and craning my neck to see where the shot had come from. I noticed two snipers, one who'd suddenly appeared high up on the fire escape landing of a neighboring apartment building and another, shooting from the second-story window of the abandoned factory behind our parking lot. I'd underestimated these guys; they'd been planning a turkey-shoot all along, and we were the turkeys. This meant they'd also be ready for us out front, so my only hope was rocketing out of there and getting past whatever barricade they'd planned to trap us in the driveway that connected the parking lot with the street.

I floored it as I raced down the driveway, but once I got to the sidewalk, I noticed not only the two front guys heading towards the car, guns drawn, aimed at the passenger side, but a large SUV that suddenly veered in front of me, blocking me from turning on to the street. I was calculating how I might possibly evade it, but the side of the SUV was practically touching the front of my car and I didn't have enough room to work with.

Just then, the SUV was literally hurled out of the way, rear-ended by a school bus. As the bus then quickly drove off, making my way clear, I tried to figure out what had just happened. Maybe the bus driver didn't see the SUV stop short until it was too late. But the SUV had veered well out of its lane onto the sidewalk. The bus could've easily passed it and continued to the intersection. But the bus had hit the SUV squarely in the back, propelling it almost halfway down the street. That was also too much force for the speed he should have been going. Somewhere in that equation, momentum was created that shouldn't have been.

I didn't have time to consider the scientific ramifications of mass and velocity because my thoughts were suddenly interrupted by gunshots. Every bit of academy training kicked in, and I felt like I was going through motions I'd rehearsed a million times before, because I had. The seemingly endless hours of instruction and repetition were designed for this and this alone: that under threat, I would immediately, unthinkingly respond in the most successful way possible.

And I did. I turned in the direction from which the bus had come and sped off. I ran two red lights and got on the highway. I figured we'd be safe there for a few minutes.

"We made it," I said. "You can come out now."

The genealogist sat up tentatively, looking around in fear. He was shaking, but I told him to take deep breaths. Then I reminded myself that I wasn't supposed to be an agent. I was grateful he hadn't been able to see my escape maneuvering. I tried to sound like a very rattled and slightly indignant civilian who'd miraculously survived a harrowing experience.

"What the hell was *that* about?!" I cried. "Those guys were *shooting* at us! We could've been *killed*!"

"I'm sorry," he said. "I didn't have anyone else to go to."

"Listen, I'm going to stay on the highway for a little bit and then I'll take you to my place, but I need to know what this is all about," I said, adding enough animation to my voice so that I sounded more than a little hysterical.

He took a deep breath and gravely began to explain that a few months earlier, he'd been approached by a federal agent. He wasn't told much about the circumstances of why he'd be doing what he'd be doing, but the authorities wanted him to do some genealogical tracing using DNA databases to match blood found at a crime scene.

He told me that this kind of request, while uncommon, sometimes came up in his line of work. He was capable of doing genealogical forensics, such as finding long-lost parents, children, siblings, half-siblings, and, in the context of criminal justice cases, finding relatives of a murder suspect at large, for instance, who might be able to shed light on their identity or whereabouts. He wasn't always successful, since only a certain percentage of the population have ever even done genealogical DNA testing, but it was always an option worth pursuing as a last resort. On several notable occasions, it had been extremely successful.

What he was telling me made sense, but for some reason, I found it hard to believe the authorities had gone to a professional genealogy company, just like anyone else. It seemed more likely that they'd have their own people on the inside who were trained for that kind of thing and who knew information security protocols, but again, that wasn't really my area of expertise. Maybe the feds having chosen to work with a civilian was an error of judgment that had caused this whole mess in the first place.

He told me that he was able to provide family contacts for the authorities of whosever blood it was that was found at the crime scene by tracing family trees and researching vital statistics documents, but that now some kind of syndicated crime organization was after him for having done so.

It was a classic case of a man who knew too much. He'd helped authorities obtain information they could use to find the criminal, and now the criminal's associates wanted him dead. Plenty of stupidity to go around, as usual, from the syndicate's misguided thirst for revenge to the authorities' incompetent protection of the genealogist. However, it did make me realize that the feds might've arranged the bus that permitted our escape.

"Did they promise you any kind of protection for doing this work?" I asked. He seemed at a loss for an answer, so I told him about the bus. He was visibly shocked.

I continued, "I guess the police—or whoever—are keeping an eye on you. They must know the mob is after you."

He paused a long time before saying, "Yes, I guess they are."

"In that case," I offered, "All you have to do is contact the federal agency that hired you. Maybe they can hide you for a while." In reality, I knew they'd have to enroll him in the Witness Protection Program, considering the ferocity with which he was hunted down today, but most people react badly when they're told that, so I left that part out. Besides, I didn't want to seem like I knew a lot about things federal agencies did.

I was about to get into the right-hand lane and take the next exit, then head back in the opposite direction towards my apartment, when my glance into the rear-view mirror revealed several black SUVs closing in on me quickly. They were still some distance away but they were moving fast.

Something wasn't making sense. I'd chalked this situation up to an ill-advised mob hit attempt on the genealogist for which the feds were only minimally prepared. Now I had an armada of what I was certain were specialized professional killers just seconds behind me. I instantly regretted my choice of car for this assignment. I didn't think a hair stylist driving a highly engineered sports car would be believable—not on my salary, anyway—so I chose a dependable used sedan with good gas mileage. It worked fine, but it was not the vehicle for what I'd need in the next few minutes. I don't think I'd ever even driven it over 60 miles an hour.

I'd been planning to call the bureau for help once I got home, but now I realized it was too late for that. The black SUVs were almost on me. I'd have to manage. More importantly, I'd have to protect my client's life, which wasn't going to be easy. The only weapons I had were the gun in my glove-compartment and the retractable garrote-wire in my wristwatch, which could obviously only be used at close range. (One of the few stereotypically secret-agent accessories with which we were provided.)

I tried to enumerate my allies. There was another agent working an assignment about thirty minutes away, but I didn't have thirty minutes to get to him. In fact, I was already out of time.

The black cars caught up to me. I was plagued with a familiar feeling that always attended moments of great decisiveness: that I wasn't going to make it. I wasn't enough; I wasn't capable. I was a failure. Somewhere in the back of my mind, I could hear my father's voice, and it infuriated me.

"Keep your head down and hang on," I shouted at my client.

I slammed on the gas, jerking the steering wheel to the right and nearly losing control of the car as I took the exit, which, by that point, we'd almost passed. I'd bought myself a few precious seconds as the SUVs screeched and spun around to follow us. I'd need every last one of them.

Once we got partway up the exit ramp, I slammed on the breaks, yelling, "Get out!" to the client as I removed my gun from the glove-compartment. I threw the car into park and had him follow me over the short barrier to a drainage culvert below that went under the exit road. It was about ten feet high and pretty long, so there was plenty of room for us to run. I'd noticed it in the past and realized that at this moment, it would make a good escape route.

Shortly after we made it into the culvert, I heard the screeching of brakes, so I knew the syndicate wasn't far behind. They were on the exit ramp, undoubtedly getting out of their cars. We'd be easy targets if we stayed in the culvert much longer.

I was in better shape than the genealogist so I outran him to the far end. We'd have to climb up onto the road and run into a nearby strip mall unless I figured out something else first, which I hoped I could do, because the genealogist wasn't doing a very good job of running.

"Hurry!" I ordered, running back towards him. "When you get out, stay low and head for the mall. I'll cover you."

He passed me and I drew my gun, knowing they'd start shooting at us in a moment, first from the part of the culvert we'd entered, and soon from the exiting side, as the men pursuing us made their way across to it.

Sure enough, someone appeared at the mouth of the culvert and fired at me. I fired back only once, realizing I'd need to save ammunition. I just wanted him to know we weren't going to be easy to catch. I also wanted to hit him, but my eyes hadn't adjusted to the darkness yet. He disappeared for a moment and I looked back to see that the genealogist had made it out the other side.

"Look!" he said, motioning me over. "I found something!"

I raced to meet him and sure enough, off to one side, there was a slightly raised manhole cover, almost totally obscured by weeds and brush overgrowth, which I'd missed in my quick assessment of the area since I'd been so focused on the strip mall across the street. We got it open and crawled in quickly. I sent him down first and pulled the cover closed after us. If I'd missed seeing it, maybe the men following us would, too. They'd assume we were sneaking our way across the street or possibly suspect we'd been picked up by a sympathetic motorist.

Still, I knew we had to move fast. I had no idea where the tunnel led, but I wanted to put a lot of distance between the mob and us. Distance was the only advantage we had.

We were walking quickly about ankle-deep in water but I didn't even notice because now I had a new problem: the genealogist asked me why I had a gun.

"I bought it illegally," I lied. "For personal protection."

"Oh," he said. He was evidently aware of hate crimes against gays, as he didn't seem to require any further explanation, so I'd managed to maintain my cover yet again.

We half-walked, half-jogged for about two minutes until we came to the end of the line: the only way out. I was guessing it would locate us somewhere near the strip mall. We'd still be pretty close to our adversaries, so we couldn't take any chances.

I gave the genealogist my pocket comb and told him to run it through his hair, which was all over the place. I didn't want to attract attention by looking any more crazed than we already probably did. Meanwhile, I untucked my shirt so it would conceal my gun, which I'd slide into my belt after we got out.

I went up the ladder and carefully lifted the manhole cover enough to see where we were. It was an active traffic intersection on one end of the strip mall. We'd be in danger of getting hit by a car, so I carefully raised the manhole cover enough to see that nobody was coming, and then quickly slid it aside, climbed out, and helped the genealogist onto the street. We practically dove into a nearby clump of dense landscaping bushes. It would be getting dark soon, so we'd be harder to spot.

I scanned the area for the black SUVs.

"Do you see them?" the genealogist asked.

"No," I said, "But that doesn't mean they aren't there. I think we'll be safe here for a little while, though."

I sat back for a moment in the warm mulch. I exercised regularly, but now that the adrenaline rush was over, I was feeling pretty spent. It's not every day I have to run for my life. The genealogist looked pale and frightened.

"It'll be okay," I said, reassuringly. "We evaded them and now we just have to get you into the hands of the authorities. Do you have the contact info for the federal people who hired you?"

The genealogist said nothing. Suddenly, I recognized the look on his face. I'd seen it too many times before not to recognize it. It was the expression of a suspect who doesn't want to talk.

CHAPTER 3

When he finally did speak, he said, "We've got to get to Texas."

"Texas?!" I exploded, sitting bolt upright. "What the hell's in Texas? Look, what's going on here?"

As darkness fell, and fewer and fewer cars passed us, he explained, very reluctantly, that it wasn't the authorities who had hired him. Not exactly.

He'd been approached by a representative of someone very wealthy and powerful. I'd tell you who, but I can't. But he told me.

This individual had a son who had been involved in a few grisly high-profile murder investigations. I was familiar with the case as I'd read about it in the news. So had everyone in the entire country. While the son was at first considered a suspect, the police couldn't prove anything. The killer's DNA had been found at two crime scenes in the form of semen and blood, but the young man didn't have a record (thanks to family intervention when he'd previously committed lesser crimes). They didn't yet have enough evidence to demand a DNA test, and were worried about a lawsuit, so the authorities decided to see if they could find any connections through family genealogy websites. If they could match the DNA to individuals with the same last name as the young man, or to whom he was otherwise related, they'd have grounds to arrest him.

As I suspected, he said the feds rarely used private genealogists, that normally they had their own people do it, but someone high up was able to divert the job to him via this hired representative of the family. So the genealogist's job was to find out if any revealing genetic information existed, and if so, to provide realistic misinformation to law enforcement so they'd be off on a wild goose-chase. It would be made to look like his results had come from within the bureau, and after investigating the leads, the police would be no closer to finding the killer, which is exactly what the killer's father wanted.

Instead of being an informer, the genealogist was actually an unwilling mis-informer, working on behalf of the killer.

"I'm very ashamed now that I did it," the genealogist sadly explained. "It was a lot of money and it was easy. I figured if anyone ever found out and questioned the results, I could just say that I got it wrong, so it wouldn't seem intentional. It's easy to make mistakes in genealogy."

My head was still reeling.

“What the hell possessed you to do something like that?” I asked. I never would’ve figured him for the shady type.

He sighed heavily and then he answered. “I’m almost fifty and I haven’t done anything worthwhile with my life. I’m tired of being unsuccessful. I figured I could retire early on the money, maybe go live on an island somewhere,” he trailed off and I could tell he was fantasizing about drinking rum out of a pineapple on a beach with pretty girls in bikinis flocking around him. Like all straight men, he was delusional.

“And meanwhile a serial-killer would remain at large. Brilliant,” I chided.

“I thought about that part afterwards,” he said. “It was just a matter of falling back into an old way of thinking. Listen, I didn’t grow up like you or like most people. My dad was a criminal. Believe it or not, that’s the life I was trained for, but I didn’t want any part of it. That’s why I took off and moved to Chicago and got an education and a professional job. That’s why I don’t have any family I can turn to right now. I’m sorry I got you involved, but you’re the only friend I’ve got.”

My mind raced back to where everything started. So the men outside the shop had been federal agents; the men on the highway had been federal agents, too. I was running away from my own colleagues who probably didn’t know I was one of them because I was deep under cover. Christ, I’d even shot at one of them in the culvert. Thank God I’d probably missed. I reasoned that they must’ve discovered that the DNA investigation was diverted outside the bureau and wanted the real information before the guy who diverted everything had a chance to pawn off the fake results and kill the genealogist. It made sense.

“Wait a minute,” I said, remembering the school bus that had cleared the path for our escape. “If we’ve been running from the feds, who was that with the bus trying to help us?”

“Must’ve been the killer’s people. They’re trying to get to me before the feds do so they can get me out of the country and make sure nobody ever finds out who that DNA really belongs to,” he said.

“Great,” I said bitterly, realizing that we were being pursued by both the feds and the killer’s hired guns. “So what exactly do you know?” I asked.

“Well, since he’s part of a famous dynasty, the killer’s family tree is well-known enough that the genetic match instantly brought it up. I’d read about the murders in the news, and how the boy was a suspect. So that’s how I understood why I was asked to make it look like the DNA traced back to a different family. But at this point, nobody knows where the boy is. The family's hiding him. I was able to find out that there's a woman in Texas who's a cousin of the killer. She comes from one of the less overexposed branches of the family and they're not as rich. She might know where he is, and maybe she'd be willing to tell us. If I could present that plus my DNA evidence to the feds, they'd have him. I've got to talk to her," he said.

I was silent for a moment as I digested this information. Then I reached two conclusions. First, the fact that the feds were even after him meant that whoever the high-ranking official was who had engineered the switch from a bureau genealogist to this guy wasn't powerful enough to call off the dogs, so to speak. That made me feel a little better. Also, I realized I might be able to find and uncover that official using my own connections there. He needed to be exposed, the quicker the better.

Second, if the killer's cousin in Texas wasn't already dead, she would be soon. I'd heard about cases like this and I knew there was no such thing as family loyalty with this much at stake for the boy's father's reputation. Murdering a relative who might talk wasn't unheard of. I decided not to say anything about it yet, though. And despite what the genealogist thought, the killer's father wasn't sending his men to protect him from falling into the hands of the feds. They were out to kill him.

"How long ago did you deliver the misinformation they wanted?" I asked.

"This morning," he said.

So now I knew they'd planned to kill him today.

There was so much to process mentally and I was so tired. It had been a long time since I'd done anything more than nod and smile while cutting hair. Even when I was working within the auspices of the bureau, I'd rarely taken part in anything this dangerous and exhausting.

I made a decision: I'd briefly hold off on contacting my agency until I had a better idea of the extent of the corruption. It probably wasn't much, but there was no use taking chances when this guy's life depended on it. We'd need to continue evading both the feds and the killer's agents, and get ourselves to Texas to see if the serial killer's cousin could tell us anything, assuming her own family hadn't already disposed of her. It was a lot of hypotheticals.

The time seemed to pass quickly. Now that it was almost fully dark and I hadn't seen a trace of the men who were chasing us, I emerged from the greenery.

"Come on," I said. "We're going to Union Station."

CHAPTER 4

Taking a train seemed to be the safest thing. There were more places to hide than on a bus, and I knew they'd be looking for us in a car. Taking a plane was too confining; we'd be easy targets when we landed.

We were about a fifteen-minute drive from Union Station. Walking would've been the safest way to get there, especially at night when we could conceal ourselves more easily, but I wanted to get on that train before the feds shared our identities with transportation officials. I decided to take the rail line downtown, then we could get on a train bound for Austin.

I explained the plan.to the genealogist.

As we rode towards the city, I kicked myself for being so gullible. Why had I believed the genealogist when he told me the syndicate was after him? I had assumed he was being honest and that he wasn't the type that would sell out. I also realized that in all my calculations pertaining to this case, I was working from only one information source—the genealogist—which was a very dangerous mistake to make in this game.

I realized that I'd have to do better. I hadn't been on my pins in a long time and this situation required me to be in top form. I resolved to sharpen up.

When we got to Union Station, I bought the tickets because nobody was looking for me, so my name wouldn't raise any red flags. We had an hour to kill before our train, so I suggested we pick up the few things we'd need. We separated but I kept an eye on him as I purchased a phone charger and a portable electric razor. I also bought a duffel bag as well as a sportscoat. I didn't know if I'd wind up doing any shooting in public. When a guy in a blazer points a gun, you figure he's a good guy; when a guy in a hoodie does, you assume he's a criminal. It was just something to ensure my image was the right one if things got ugly.

The genealogist offered to get coffee for us. By the way, I'm obviously not at liberty to tell you his real name, but for simplicity's sake, let's just call him "Charlie." So Charlie went to get coffee and I bought a couple of magazines. We had a twenty-eight hour trip ahead of us, so I definitely wanted reading material.

Minutes later, Charlie returned looking drunk, although I knew nobody could get so drunk that quickly. He handed me the coffees and practically stumbled into me in the process. I helped him to a bench; something was wrong with him. He could barely hold his head up or keep his eyes open.

"Charlie," I said, "Did you drink any coffee?"

"Yeah," he slurred. "The one with the open lid."

I grabbed the cup and took a look; there was some light foaming on the surface of the coffee. He'd been drugged. Mine was probably drugged too.

"Did you leave them unattended?" I asked.

"Only for a minute while I . . . "

He couldn't even finish the sentence. It was probably gamma-hydroxybutyrate. It wouldn't have been difficult for someone to discreetly splash some in the cups. He'd be asleep in no time.

I looked around. Whoever did it must be watching. I threw the coffees into a trash can and scanned the room. At that moment, two men rounded a corner and headed straight for me.

"Your friend doesn't look well," one of them said, putting his hand around my arm. "Here, let us help you get him home." He stood close enough to me that I knew he had a gun in his jacket pocket.

The other one pulled Charlie up and they started hustling us towards the exit very quickly. I felt sure there'd be a car waiting for us, and it wouldn't be a federal vehicle. Once we got in, we'd be out of options, so I had to make sure that didn't happen.

I had to draw a crowd. It wasn't the best plan, but it was the only one I could think of quickly.

I unzipped my trousers and pulled them, and my underwear, down to my knees.

Nudity freaks everyone out. Men stared. Women screamed. Parents dragged their children away. Even our captors were startled.

I saw a security guard come running, so I started slapping my hands against my shins. By the time he reached me, the two guys were gone and I said to the guard, "Thank goodness you're here! A mouse ran up my pants leg! I think he's still trapped in there!"

"You've gotta pull those up right now, sir—right now," he said sternly.

"I'm really sorry," I said, looking rattled and still shaking out my pants legs, "I just can't stand mice and I can't believe the damn thing ran up my pants like that," adding, "Oh my God, I must've made a scene. I'm really, really sorry." I quickly hiked my pants back up and zipped them, commenting, "You know, you really need to get pest control in here—a rodent problem like that is a public health hazard."

It was all Charlie could do not to fall over since I'd let go of him, and he was about to collapse, so I bolstered him and said, "My friend's had a little too much to drink. We're waiting for our train and train-travel makes him anxious; he thought it would calm his nerves."

"You sure he's the only one who's been drinking?" the guard asked suspiciously.

Fortunately, my story had been just crazy enough that there wasn't any trouble, but the guard wanted to make sure we got on the train, so he escorted us to the platform, for which I was grateful. The guys who'd tried to kidnap us were nowhere to be found.

Still, they knew we were there in the first place, so they must've followed us. Either that or they had people posted at all the transit venues.

Before I knew it, an enthusiastic redcap helped me get Charlie (who was basically unconscious by that point) onto the train and into our private room.

After I locked the door and pulled down the window shade, I felt somewhat better.

CHAPTER 5

Later that night as I sat, pretending to read a magazine article I'd been staring at for ten minutes while Charlie looked out the window, having mostly recovered from being drugged, I realized that our room on the train was the safest place to be as we made our way to Texas. The seats were comfortable for riding during the day, and at night, they converted into two sleeping berths—one above the other—like bunk beds. There was a small toilet and sink in the compartment. I could have our meals delivered by the porter.

The train made occasional stops, but I could keep the door locked and I was armed. As far as I knew, the authorities didn't know we were aboard; only the killer's hired men did.

Now that I was safely settled in, my mind relaxed and I could think deeply. I had a lot of major obstacles. I had to figure out who in the bureau was both powerful enough and crooked enough to have engineered this ruse requiring bad information from the genealogist. I also had to figure out what we were going to do once we got to Texas in search of the killer's cousin, who might be dead or reluctant to talk, neither of which would be helpful to the situation, assuming we could even find her in the first place.

Little details from earlier in the day started coming to mind, such as the missed first shot which had been taken at us in the parking lot of the salon. The feds had missed on purpose; it was a warning shot to scare us into surrendering. The same with the officer who'd shot at me in the culvert. Those guys, the ones they send for that kind of work, are crack shots and wouldn't have missed if they didn't mean to.

But what started bothering me was what a bad job they were doing of catching Charlie. We're all human, and I'm not saying we never make mistakes, but this seemed unusually sloppy for a government entity of this stature. The more I thought about it, I shouldn't have been able to abscond with Charlie if he were being adequately tracked. It hadn't been easy, but it should've been impossible. This wasn't like them. There was something else going on, maybe having to do with whatever corrupt element was at work in the system.

I drew a deep breath. This was a complicated mess and I had a civilian's life in my hands. I couldn't count on anyone on the inside since I didn't know whom I could trust. Involving friends or family was out of the question.

I set up the sleeping berths and after making him drink some water, I helped Charlie, who was still groggy, into the upper berth. He'd be safe up there and I could guard the door from the lower bunk. I slipped my gun under my pillow and turned off the light. I'd need to get some rest and this would be the best time to do it, while the situation was still so fresh that the people who were after us would not have yet mobilized into an invincible force, which they might yet do tomorrow.

Before my mind could start contemplating that possibility, I remembered a verse from the Sermon on the Mount that my grandmother used to quote whenever she was facing a challenge: "Sufficient unto the day is the evil thereof."

I closed my eyes and went to sleep.

CHAPTER 6

The next morning, I awoke early, folded away my sleeping berth, and washed up at the sink. I gave myself a shave with the electric razor and put on a fresh shirt which I'd also bought at Union Station. In addition, I washed some of our things in the sink so we'd have a change of clothes when we arrived in Texas. One of my teachers at the academy impressed upon us the importance of looking neat. Beyond the discipline of personal hygiene, being presentable increased our chances of being favorably considered during that split-second during which the average person decides if someone is trustworthy. Serial killers know this, which is why they're able to win people's confidence by appearing well-groomed, well-spoken, and charming. I knew that if Charlie or I should need someone's help, it would be good not to look too bedraggled.

Charlie woke up right around the time I was finishing up. He said he felt okay but I was still worried about him. I told him I'd get our breakfast and made him swear not to let me back into the compartment unless he heard me give the "Shave and a Haircut" knock.

Charlie laughed. "That's pretty funny," he said, "I mean, coming from you."

At first, I didn't have a clue what he meant, but then I got the joke. As I walked down the narrow train corridor, it seemed like a million years since I'd been a hair stylist. His remark was a good reminder that I couldn't afford to forget my cover.

Checking my watch, I realized it would be time for me to show up at the salon in an hour, so I made a quick call to Rosa, who was nearly hysterical and passed the phone to Lola, the owner. Lola was worried I'd been hurt in the previous day's shootout. I told her I hadn't seen any of it, that I'd already been on my way at the time and it must've taken place just after I'd left. She said they'd called me several times to check on me and I hadn't answered, but I explained that I'd taken a hot bath and gone straight to bed and fallen into a deep sleep, which dovetailed nicely with a lie that what I'd mistaken for a hangover was actually the beginning of the flu, and I wouldn't be at work for several days. Clearly relieved I was safe, Lola happily agreed to reschedule my appointments and urged me to rest as long as I needed. I was lucky she was such a kind lady, and I was touched by how worried she and Rosa had sounded. In my line of work, you try not to get emotionally attached, but I was genuinely fond of both of them. At any rate, now my cover was safe on that front for a couple of days.

Moments later, while I was buying breakfast, I took a good look around and decided there was nothing of concern going on. I returned to our room and Charlie let me in.

We ate with great appetite because we hadn't had dinner the night before. I was grateful for the hot coffee to stimulate my mind and energize me.

When we were done eating, Charlie napped lightly in his seat while I pretended to read a magazine and set to work figuring out the main problems in the situation, which had now expanded to include a question I hadn't even considered last night: was it realistic of me to assume the feds even knew about Charlie? Considering they thought some internal forensic genealogist was doing the work, how did they become aware of Charlie's existence? His inclusion in the investigation was an irregularity that had been secretly arranged by the killer's contact, high up in the agency. Unless there had been an internal investigation (which usually took a while, and what would've prompted it?) it was unlikely they knew about him and wanted to get the real DNA info from him.

I almost couldn't believe I'd missed that crucial fact in the jumble of circumstances and alliances, but when mixed liberally with pressure and fear, these things happen, especially when you're as rusty as I was. Also, even when I'd been working on the inside, I rarely dealt with anything remotely like this. My work was always behind a desk or in an interrogation room.

Although I couldn't extrapolate all the details, it seemed someone was protecting Charlie, or at least trying to. That was a comforting thought. Then again, it meant that there were people I could trust in the agency and those I couldn't—the problem was I didn't know which were which.

Still, if the feds were protecting Charlie from the killer's people, he'd be in the news. They'd be trying to bring him in. I looked up from my magazine.

"Can you check and see if there are any news reports about us?" I asked. Charlie picked up his phone and started researching. After a few minutes of scanning, he said there was nothing. I found that strange. Surely there'd be some kind of news blurb about us, maybe even planted to get us to turn ourselves in to the non-corrupt agents who were keeping an eye on us. Then again, Charlie was a consummate researcher so I trusted he'd missed nothing.

My thoughts then turned to our destination. "Where in Texas is this cousin of the killer's?" I asked.

"A little town called Fredericksburg," he said. "It's in central Texas, about an hour from Austin, where we'll be getting off."

At least we wouldn't have too far to travel. But I didn't like the idea of a small town, especially out in the middle of nowhere. That meant it would be easier for the killer's men to have already finished off the cousin. There was something to be said for having neighbors who could serve as witnesses to a crime. I'd never been to Texas, but from what I'd heard, it could be a mile between homes out in the country. Screams don't carry that far.

"And you're sure this is the one who's the DNA match?" I asked.

"As sure as I can be," Charlie said. "She has an unusual name and her online family tree mentioned her as living in Fredericksburg, Texas. I could be wrong, but I don't think so." I knew he was experienced and I didn't doubt his results.

I went back to magazine-reading and contemplated trying to get word to some of my connections at the department. I couldn't risk contacting them directly. Then again, I had to make sure someone knew what was going on.

Just then, there was a knock at the door of our room.

Charlie looked at me nervously, but I just put my finger to my lips to indicate he should remain quiet. I got up, went to the door without opening it, and asked who it was.

"I'm the porter, sir. I think you dropped some money out here," came a deep voice from the other side.

I put my hand in my pocket and sure enough, it was empty. I'd had two twenties left over from buying breakfast that weren't there.

I opened the door and thanked the porter, who handed me the money, saying he found it on the floor just outside the door. I took a quick look in his eyes. He didn't look away, and the sides of his mouth turned up slightly. He was an honest man. He easily could've made off with the forty bucks, but he didn't.

I told him how embarrassed I was for having been so careless, and introduced myself. He told me his name was Ambrose. He looked about sixty and was extremely dignified. I could tell he was an old-school porter, the kind that seem to have an innate sense of what train-travelers need and the ability to provide it quickly and efficiently. Men like Ambrose gave some of the best service anywhere in the country. Generations before, their forerunners had been formerly enslaved men hired by George Pullman to serve passengers on his famous Pullman train cars, and over the years, working as a train porter became a highly coveted job for African-American men, as it gave them the unique opportunity to travel all across America.

I decided that Ambrose could be counted upon in an emergency, even if I weren't running for my life. I'd noticed him in the coach section on my way to get breakfast, calming a fussy baby with an animal cracker, to the immense relief of the child's overwrought mother.

A strange, knowing look passed across Ambrose's face. "Is there anything else I can do for you?" he asked.

"No," I said. "We're fine, my friend and I. Just getting a little rest on the way to Austin."

"Well, if you need anything, you just let me know," he said, nodding as he strode down the corridor.

I assured him I would and went back inside, locking the door behind me.

CHAPTER 7

By noon, we still had about thirteen hours to go until we arrived in Texas. I brought some sandwiches back to our room and we ate them silently. I think we were both still rattled by the previous day's events. Sometimes it takes a while for things to hit you.

After lunch, I decided to write up a short note explaining our circumstances. I addressed it to one of my colleagues back at the department. He was one of the nicer guys I'd worked with. We went out after work for drinks occasionally. He had a pretty wife and two small children. He'd always struck me as trustworthy, so I couldn't imagine him being part of any corruption at the bureau.

I was about to stick the note in the inner pocket of my blazer when the train slowed to a stop. I'd been keeping track of the various stations, but we weren't due to arrive at one for quite a while.

"Stay here," I said to Charlie, stepping out into the corridor. I happened to see Ambrose at the end of the car, and he came towards me at once.

"Why are we stopping?" I asked.

"They're telling us it's something about trouble with a fuel line," he said slowly. He didn't have to say any more. I could tell by the tone of his voice that he didn't believe it. Ambrose had to have been riding the trains for decades. He knew the kinds of problems they routinely encountered.

He said, "Sir, if you'll allow, you and your friend might want to come with me to the kitchen. The chef just made a new recipe and needs volunteers to try it."

The man was clairvoyant, I could've sworn.

"We'd be glad to help," I said. I ducked into the compartment and hustled Charlie out and down the corridor, as fast as we could follow Ambrose, who was striding swiftly. We made it through several cars until we entered the kitchen, which was a gleaming spectacle of stainless-steel cupboards and counters. Ambrose led us carefully through the galley-style setup, weaving our way among men busily chopping salads and stirring soups until we got to a pantry of sorts with a clothing rack opposite. He pulled down a couple of caps and aprons for us to wear.

Looking around suspiciously, he remarked, "Guests in the kitchen always wear the proper attire, that's the rules," so we quickly put them on. Then he told us to wait in the pantry until the chef could serve us, so we'd be out of the way of the cooks. He got no argument from me as he closed the door so only a hint of light was coming through.

"What's this about?" Charlie whispered.

"Something's going on; something that isn't usual." I told him. "Ambrose—the porter—he knows we're in trouble and he's helping us. Just play along."

After that we just stood silently. It was pretty nerve-wracking. We must've been in that pantry for fifteen minutes before he finally came to get us. As he spoke, the train began moving again.

"I'm so sorry, gentlemen," he announced, holding his hand out for our caps and aprons. "Chef says the chowder's not fit to try. The cream curdled. Must've been spoiled but he didn't know it until he added it into the pot. Sometimes you never know until you put it in hot water. That's when you find out the truth about things."

He offered to escort us back to our compartment, and we followed him. I noticed he checked each car while we stood back until he motioned us to come through.

When we got back and Charlie was inside, he confirmed my fears by quietly saying, "Funny thing at that last stop, four passengers got on even though there's no station. Big gentlemen, wearing suits." Ambrose and I exchanged looks.

I reached into my pocket and pulled out the letter.

"This is a letter I'm supposed to mail once I get to Austin, but I'm afraid I'll forget. Would you mind giving this back to me and reminding me once we get there? And if I somehow manage to get off the train without you noticing, do you think you could drop it in a mailbox for me? It's very important," I said.

"I'll make sure," he said, taking the letter. For a split second I thought about telling him who I was, but it wouldn't have made a difference. He was already on my side. I wondered what gave me away. Probably something tiny yet significant that only a porter would know. It occurred to me that my office might do better recruiting from the legions of train porters than from Quantico.

Back in the compartment, I considered keeping Charlie in the dark about the four new passengers but it would be safer if he knew what was really going on so he could react quickly if need be. We might be facing situations where every second would count.

After I told him, he asked me what we should do.

"Just stay in here and stay quiet," I said. "We should be fine. The killer's men are probably hoping to catch us out of the compartment or getting off the train at Austin."

"How'll we get past them there?" he asked.

"I don't know yet, but I'll think of something," I said.

The problem with this kind of situation, I realized, is that you get difficulty on top of difficulty just at a time when you have the least bandwidth to deal with everything. I checked my watch: just under twelve hours until Austin.

Suddenly, it seemed like the train was slowing down again. Certain I must be wrong—hoping I was—I turned to Charlie and was about to ask him if he felt it too, when I heard some kind of metallic snapping sound at the door and before I knew it, two men rushed in and grabbed us. They taped our mouths shut, tied our hands behind our backs and hurried us down the corridor. There, I saw the two others, one of whom was making a phone call.

As I was shoved down the steps and off the train, Charlie behind me, one of the guys took my gun, which I'd tucked into the back of my pants. They were very quick and very efficient. Whoever hired them, they mustn't have come cheap. They knew what they were doing.

We were bundled into a van which sped off, but not before they put hoods over our faces so we couldn't see anything. Since he was sitting next to me, I kept one leg touching Charlie's leg so I could keep track of him.

Believe it or not, having a bag over my head and being deprived of stimuli made for great thinking. Even at school, I always used to study better with the shades drawn and no noise. The four guys hadn't said a word. They were probably communicating with signals. Definitely very well trained.

I briefly ran through my status: no weapon, unable to see, speak, or move, and being transported against my will in a van. With a civilian in tow. The best thing I could do would be to figure out what they wanted with us and where we were going, and I would've done just that, except that's when they knocked me unconscious.

CHAPTER 8

When I came to, I could tell I was lying on the ground outdoors. The earth has a certain comforting feel to it, which was a welcome contrast to the pain in my head. I could smell soil and a slight mossiness. I gathered I was in a forest somewhere. The bag was still over my head and everything was quiet for a moment, then I heard the sound of a gunshot about 50 yards away. Then another.

I flinched instinctively as if I'd been punched in the gut. All I could think was that they were executing Charlie. The thought immediately flashed through my mind that he'd died on my watch. It horrified me, and at the same time, I could feel the familiar sting of my father's disapproval, even though he'd been dead for years.

I'd screwed up. It had cost a man his life.

Before I could start cataloging where I'd gone wrong, or what I might have done differently, I heard a car door slam, and then the sound of footsteps approaching as the car drove away.

Someone silently began untying my hands and removed the bag from my face.

It was Charlie.

"What happened?!" I asked, jumping to my feet. In the distance, I saw the bodies of two of our captors.

"I don't know," he said. "I only came to a moment ago when I heard the shots. Then two guys untied me, jumped in the car, and took off."

"What did they look like?" I asked eagerly. "What kind of car was it?"

"I don't know," he said, looking confused. "My head's really messed up. I guess I didn't notice."

"Did you hear them say anything?" I asked, becoming frustrated.

"They might've said something; I don't remember," he said, putting his hand to the side of his head and wincing.

There were more questions I wanted to ask, but I caught myself and remembered I was supposed to be a plucky hairdresser, not a government agent. I thought maybe I'd try again later; by then his memory might clear up a bit.

I went over to check on the two captors and they were definitely dead. It was a professional kill, one bullet each. I searched them for weapons, but didn't find anything. I also checked for ID but there was none. Someone had already cleaned them out, probably whoever killed them.

"Hey, don't pick their pockets," Charlie admonished.

I was about to explain that I was looking for identification, but instead realized it would be more prudent for my cover to go with his assumption and said, "Well, we don't have any money, and they sure won't be needing it."

"Come on," Charlie said, "Let's get out of here."

"There must be a road somewhere since they got here by car," I said, trying to follow their tracks, which disappeared into a clearing. After that, I couldn't find a trace. Tracking had never been my strong suit.

I knew we had to get away fast in case anyone came, which was ironic, considering we needed help. I decided to go a short distance, hide out, and then assess our options.

I figured Charlie would feel better if he thought I knew what I was doing, so I confidently directed "This way," and we both moved quickly along in my chosen direction for about five minutes until we found a secluded thicket.

"Let's catch our breath here," I said, sitting down. Charlie joined me, wiping the perspiration from his forehead.

As far as I knew, we could be anywhere, but most likely Arkansas. It might be a while before we came across a town. It also meant the days would be warm despite it being early October, but the nights would be cold.

Watching Charlie continue to perspire, I realized we needed to find a water source. I also tried to gauge his anxiety level. It seemed the farther we walked, the more worried he'd become.

"Where the hell are we?" he asked.

"Probably Arkansas. Don't worry; we're safe. We'll find food and set up a shelter later on. It might be a little while until we hit civilization, but we'll make it," I said in an encouraging voice.

"How are we going to get to Texas?" he asked.

"I don't know yet, but I'll figure something out. Remember, I'm the creative one," I joked, in an attempt to lighten the mood.

Charlie smiled a little.

I quipped, "I wish this could all be fixed with a dab of product and a roller brush, but we'll manage."

I took stock of our situation. Everything we'd had, except for the note I'd given Ambrose—and thank God for that—was in the train compartment. We had no money, no weapons, no shelter, no cellphones, and worst of all, no water. And we had no idea where the nearest town was. I tried to think positively. At least none of the people pursuing us could find us since even we didn't know where we were. As for the mysterious men who killed our captors, whoever they were and whoever they were working for, they clearly didn't want us dead or we'd have already been killed. Overall, as odd as the situation was, you could say we were ahead of the game.

Getting Charlie to work on a task would be a good way to occupy his mind and keep him from fretting, so I told him to find us two walking-sticks. They would make the hiking easier and could serve as crude weapons if necessary. I'd forage for food in the meantime since we'd need something to keep up our strength.

As I walked around looking at foliage and plants, I recalled that it was impossible to be more than five miles from a road anywhere in the continental United States—except for the few particularly remote places where it *was* possible. We might be in one of them. This made all the more sense considering that whoever pulled us off the train came across as being highly trained professionals. They'd never risk bringing us to a populated area to kill us.

As I was pondering this thought, Charlie hollered "How about this?" He was pointing to a dry, thin, low tree-branch just about the right length.

“That’s perfect,” I said. “Just stand on it near the trunk and snap it with your weight.” It was low to the ground, just about two feet above it. I turned back to my foraging and heard the sound of a crisp snap and then a cry of pain.

Wheeling around, I saw Charlie sitting on the ground, clutching his ankle.

I ran over and saw that he’d hurt himself in the fall.

“I think I broke my ankle,” he wailed.

“Let me take a look at it,” I said, bending down to examine it.

“It’s not broken,” I announced, “You just sprained the hell out of it.”

“When I landed, my foot turned inwards,” he explained, panting in agony.

I exhaled sharply. This was not good. Now we wouldn’t be able to travel as quickly on foot, and, as I’d just calculated, we might have a lot more territory to cover than I’d originally anticipated. I asked myself why I hadn’t just gotten the walking sticks, but then remembered that it was to give Charlie something productive to do.

I realized that now he would be particularly unproductive due to his injury.

“I’m sorry I asked you to do that,” I said.

“It’s not your fault,” Charlie replied. “I’m just fat and clumsy.”

Something about the way he said that bothered me. I could tell he meant it. Probably he’d heard it said to him. It made me sick.

“Listen,” I said, “There’s nothing wrong with you and you were only doing your best. It was a simple accident. It could’ve happened to anyone.”

He looked at me with a strange mix of anguish and gratitude. I’d never seen that expression on his face before. In fact, most of the time, he was extraordinarily un-expressionless, which is why it struck me so much.

I could also tell he was in a lot of pain.

“Stay here,” I said, noticing a small willow tree which hadn’t been visible from where I’d been standing before. It was a godsend because it meant water was nearby, but first, I ripped off two small boughs.

I returned to Charlie, handing him one.

“Here,” I said. “Chew on that.”

He held it away from himself, looking at it skeptically.

"I'm not hungry," he said.

"It's not food," I explained. "The sap has properties that are the same as aspirin. It'll take away the pain. It'll work on our headaches, too," I added, gratefully beginning to chaw on the soft bough. My head had begun to throb.

"Look, you stay here and rest. I'll get us some water," I said.

I went back to the willow and sure enough, there was a small stream running near it. I tested the water and it was clear and fresh. After taking a drink and washing myself off, I got a large green leaf from a nearby shrub and twisted it into a makeshift conical cup. I filled it with water and brought it to Charlie, who drank it immediately. I made four more trips until he said he'd had enough. I thought he was probably still thirsty but didn't like making me run back and forth to fetch it for him.

Since he was settled comfortably, I told him to rest and I'd go back to foraging for food. I'd also have to think about making a fire soon, I realized, as the sun's angle told me it was probably close to three or four o'clock at this point. Gathering the proper tools would take some time.

About half an hour later, I returned with the food.

"What's all this?" Charlie asked when I set it down.

"Acorns and cattail heads—we can roast them. I found the cattails in a swampy area a few minutes from here. There was also a very nice persimmons tree," I said, producing half a dozen of the fruits.

Charlie looked apprehensive but kept his thoughts to himself.

"How's your ankle feeling?" I asked.

He brightened visibly.

"Much better," he said. "That stuff really worked."

"Told you," I said.

"What do we do now?" Charlie asked.

"Well, I'll find something to make a fire tonight. I was thinking of making a shelter, but it looks like mild weather. I'll just improvise something to keep us from getting chilly," I said.

After that, I went back to the stream several times with water for Charlie and had another drink for myself. I let the water run over my hands and then put them over my eyes. The coolness felt good.

Suddenly, I heard a twig snap about ten yards away. I startled. The sound hadn't come from where Charlie was. I looked but didn't see anything, so I rushed back to the thicket where I'd left him, and he wasn't there. However, I could see him wandering afar and snapping twigs.

"Charlie!" I shouted.

"Just getting some wood for the fire," he said.

I took a deep breath. My hands were shaking.

"Okay," I said. "I'll be back in a little bit."

With that, I headed off to find a dry area where I might locate some flint, but I was still shaken. I realized I'd let my guard down, relaxed by the peacefulness of the area. It was unforgivably careless of me. Here we were, miles from anything, with people after us, having just narrowly escaped with our lives. We weren't playing house. We were on the run from deadly forces, a fact which I knew I could not afford to forget again.

Geology was one of the less-interesting aspects of my survival training, but I managed to identify large amounts of shale and sandstone on the ground. What I wasn't finding was any flint. I remember my instructor telling us you could actually find it along roads since it was one of the components of gravel, but there weren't any roads around. Finally, I found a small piece, and then a very good-sized piece near it. That would do.

On the way back, I found some fading dandelions and thought about digging up the roots for dinner, but then I remembered how bitter they were and decided against it.

When I got back, Charlie had arranged a pile of twigs and had set aside some larger branches and a few chunks of wood from a rotted, dried tree that would make wonderful firewood.

"Good work," I said.

It took me about another twenty minutes to gather large rocks to put around the place where we'd start the campfire and get some dried leaves for kindling.

"Do we really need that many?" Charlie asked, seeing the large pile of leaves.

"Have you ever started a fire like this?" I asked.

"No," he answered.

"Trust me—no matter how many dry leaves you think you'll need, you'll need about five times more," I said. "Once we get the fire started, we don't want it going out."

"But isn't that what the flint's for?" he asked. "To start the fire?"

"This isn't a disposable lighter," I said, showing him the rocks in my palm. "It's a royal pain. It works, but it takes a lot to get the spark to ignite."

"Oh," he said.

"And just in case you were wondering, I don't have a squirrel on a treadmill to power a microwave to cook our dinner. This is primitive. It's going to be rough. Don't take anything for granted," I said brusquely.

As soon as I'd spoken, I realized I was getting really snippy. Being tired, stressed, and hungry had put my nerves on edge. Agents who work like this for the long haul eventually adapt; they get used to alternating between a state of high alert and low-energy watchfulness. In the last 24 hours, I'd gone from panic to unconsciousness. I'd have to mitigate my emotional extremes or I wouldn't be able to function much longer, and I had no idea how long it would be before this whole situation with Charlie was over. It could be several days more, possibly even a week or longer.

"I'm sorry," I said. "I'm just tired."

"It's okay," Charlie said.

After that, I went off to gather some pine boughs for our shelter. There were a lot of evergreens around the area where we were, but I had to walk for a while to find ones that had low-enough branches that I could access. I was able to get quite a few nice ones, and also another walking stick.

As I feared, it took a long time to start the fire. As I was trying to ignite the dry leaves, I remembered it had taken me a long time to start a fire back when I'd had survival training, too. Charlie watched with fascination. Despite my disclaimer earlier, I think he still had some idea that I was going to click two rocks together and a roaring fire would burst forth.

"That's the trouble with people today," I commented, once I'd finally got the fire going and was skewering cattails on a stick for roasting. "Nobody knows how to survive in nature. Take away electricity and cellphones and they're doomed."

"You look like you know what you're doing," Charlie commented.

"My father taught me about survival in the woods," I lied. (In reality, the only time my father spent enjoying nature was on a private golf course, but Charlie didn't need to know that.) "He was hoping to make an outdoorsman of me," I embellished. "Or any kind of man at all, I guess."

"Did he know you were—" Charlie stopped short of finishing his sentence.

"Gay?" I asked. "Not that I ever told him, but he figured it out."

"That must've been tough," he offered.

I shrugged. "He would've been harsh even if I were straight. He was very critical," I said. "You know, just that kind of person. Nothing was good enough."

Charlie nodded. Then he said, "My father and I got along well until I told him I was going straight," then realizing the joke he'd inadvertently made, he laughed. It made me laugh too.

"Maybe I should re-word that: when I told him I wasn't going to be a criminal like him," he said.

"That's a strange thing you did, I mean, given how he was," I said. "What made you decide?"

"I didn't want to be like that," he said. "I had a lot of admiration for my father—he was really good at what he did—but I guess I wanted to be like regular people."

"What did he do, if you don't mind my asking?" I said.

Suddenly, I got the "I don't want to talk" look, the way my subjects used to during interrogation. I realized I'd gone too far.

"Robbery mostly, and then he got mixed up with the mob," he said cautiously, but his voice had changed.

Shortly thereafter, we were eating our acorns and roasted cattails.

"God, these things are bitter," he said, spitting out the first few acorns he tried.

"They're good protein," I said, although he was right. "We can't eat a lot since they're raw and too many will poison us, but try to eat the few I gave you."

He dutifully chewed the one he had in his mouth.

Meanwhile, the cattails tasted like burned cucumbers. I was looking forward to having the persimmons for dessert, if only to take the lingering taste of the cattails out of my mouth.

"Aren't there berries in the woods?" Charlie asked.

"Not this time of year," I said. "They're long gone. Besides, the birds go after them like crazy."

"How about mushrooms?" he asked.

"Look, this isn't a five-star restaurant. If you were hoping for sautéed morel mushrooms, you can forget it. I don't trust myself with mushrooms—you pick the wrong one, and you can get horrifically sick. Even experienced foragers make mistakes. It's not worth the risk."

"Well how are we going to survive on this stuff?" he asked.

"We have water. That's all we really need," I told him.

"But we'll starve to death," he protested.

“No you won’t, I promise. You can go about two months without food. You won’t be doing cartwheels, but you won’t die. Most people don’t know that,” I said.

“I thought you could only go a few days without food,” he said.

“Nope,” I assured him. “Now water is different,” I explained. “You’ve got three days. That’s it.”

“Really?” he said.

“Yes. That’s why we’ll be fine as long as we have that stream,” I said. “Besides, the area is pretty marshy once you go a little bit further. We’ll be okay.”

We were both exhausted, so as soon as we finished the persimmons, we wanted to sleep.

I set us up against a big tree and covered the ground with several pine boughs and made a rudimentary lean-to.

“We’ll both sleep in it,” I said. “It’ll get cold tonight and being next to each other will keep us warm. Don’t worry; I won’t try anything. Even if I were attracted to you—which I’m not—I’m too damned tired.”

Maybe I was imagining it, but a faint look of relief crossed Charlie’s face. I’ll never figure out why straight men all assume we’re dying to jump them.

As we were settling into the lean-to, I began to hear coyotes far away, yelping in the newly fallen darkness. I dozed listening to them until an owl’s call in the tree above us woke me with a start. Charlie was still fast asleep. The owl continued to call intermittently and it made me feel safe to go back to sleep, knowing he would keep watch over us.

CHAPTER 9

As soon as I woke up, I realized the morning was going to be absolute hell without coffee.

My head still hurt, Charlie’s ankle was still causing him pain, and while I’d slept restfully enough, we were still lost in the woods and being pursued by killers. The least I deserved was a cup of coffee to fortify me for whatever lay ahead. My survival instructor had said something about using sumac, but I hadn’t bothered taking notes, assuming the last place I’d ever find myself was in the middle of the woods needing a cup of coffee. How wrong I was.

I got some more willow for us to chew on and we had a refreshing drink of water from the stream. Neither of us were particularly hungry for more foraged fare, but I decided to see if I could find any more persimmons.

While I was wandering, I heard a noise that was unmistakably human: someone burping.

I froze in my tracks.

"Well, hello there," came a low voice.

An older man appeared in the clearing ahead of me. He was wearing a cowboy hat, a short-sleeved button-up shirt, jeans, and boots.

"Just came to tell you that you can't set fires in these parts," he said.

He was wearing a sidearm but he seemed friendly.

"I don't understand," I said. His presence had completely taken me by surprise.

"No fires on the refuge," he explained.

"Refuge? Where am I?" I asked.

"Felsenthal National Wildlife Refuge," he said proudly. "Last night, I saw the smoke from your fire, so I figured I'd come up here at first light and let you know."

"Are you a park ranger?" I asked.

"No, I'm not on the refuge staff but I might as well be, I'm up here all the time," he said. "My name's Joseph Mace," he said, extending his hand. "But everyone calls me Rocky Joe."

I gave him my name and explained that a friend and I had come camping but that we were lost. I hoped he was as stupid as he looked since my story wasn't going to add up.

"You're between Eagle Creek and County Road 60," he said. "Where's your friend?"

"Back there," I said indicating Charlie's location. "He's hurt himself—twisted ankle."

"Well, let's go have a look," he said.

When we got back to camp, Charlie looked visibly startled but I quickly said, "This is Rocky Joe. He's going to help us."

"You two don't have much gear, do you?" he observed. "Always good to travel light."

"It's part of a survival training," Charlie said awkwardly. For once, I was glad he'd spoken up. I doubt I would've thought of anything that clever so early in the morning.

"Yes," I agreed. "We've just taken a course and we were hoping to see if we could manage without a compass or food or any of that—and clearly, well, we can't. It's a good thing you found us."

"You boys ain't got any food?" he asked in astonishment.

"No, we ate acorns and cattails last night. I'd kill for a cup of coffee right now," I said.

He did a quick examination of Charlie's ankle and then turned to me.

"If you think you can get him about a quarter mile that way," he said pointing in the distance in the direction where we'd been mysteriously released, "I'll bring my truck up and carry you into town."

We agreed and Charlie and I hustled to get to the road as quickly as we could. We wanted to be ready to jump into the truck so there wouldn't be any chance of Rocky Joe discovering the bodies of the men who'd kidnapped us, which were still there.

As I helped Charlie along, I realized we had a whole new set of problems. How could we explain having no money? And what about not having cellphones? Even if we were roughing it, that made no sense. Not to mention being far from home with no visible means of having been transported to the wildlife refuge.

I decided the best thing would be to keep our mouths shut. Rocky Joe struck me as one of those country types that would probably do enough talking for all of us. I just had to get him going, and that probably wouldn't be too hard.

As soon as the truck pulled up, Charlie and I got in so quickly Rocky Joe hardly had to stop at all.

"I just need to go up the Refuge Headquarters for a minute and then I can take you on down to Crossett. It's only five miles. Unless you'd rather go somewhere else," he said.

"Crossett's just fine," I said, as if I had any idea. "We really appreciate it. Maybe you can tell us the best place to get coffee."

That was all the provocation Rocky Joe needed to launch into a review of every diner within a thirty-mile radius. At one point, Charlie gave me a sidelong glance and I flashed him a small grin.

Rocky Joe's soliloquy lasted just long enough to consume the entire trip to the Refuge Headquarters, where he hopped out, saying he'd be back momentarily.

To my surprise, when he returned, he stuck his head in the window and said someone had left a message for me, and asked me to come inside.

"It'll be okay," I whispered to Charlie as I got out, although I had no such expectation. On the contrary, I figured they were going to arrest me inside for the murder of the men back in the woods, but if that were the case, they would've arrested Charlie, too. It was baffling because nobody knew we were here. Who could possibly be leaving me a message?

Once inside, Rocky Joe led me to a counter where he told a heavyset young woman, "This is the feller I was telling you about."

The woman said my name and I replied, "Yes, that's me."

She said, "This come in yesterday afternoon—it's a bulletin they sent to the police and everyone," indicating a piece of paper she was holding. "There's been a family emergency and they want you to get to your cousin Dylan's house in Mount Holly right away."

Dylan was the name of my contact in the bureau—the one to whom I'd written the letter that I'd given Ambrose, but there was no way it could've been delivered so quickly. Being blindsided by something like this wasn't what I was prepared for, but the name made me think it was some kind of attempt to save me, so I tried to roll with it.

"Oh, I see," I said, looking crestfallen. "There's only one problem. My friend and I actually hitchhiked here, so I'd have to find somewhere to rent a car if I'm going to get there quickly," I began.

"No need of that," the young woman said. "I just got off the phone with the police in Whitlow Junction. They said they'll take you there. Not every day we get a billionaire's son 'round these parts." She beamed at me.

While my family is extremely rich, we aren't billionaires, but that must've been the excuse my savior (whoever they were) concocted to justify having a manhunt for me, and why everyone was so eager to be helpful.

"I certainly am grateful to you both," I said, adding as an afterthought, "As is my family. I hope when this unfortunate situation is past, you'll allow us to make a donation to the refuge."

I turned to leave, but then had a further inspiration to capitalize on my newfound celebrity.

"Before I go, could I trouble you for a coffee for myself and my friend?"

CHAPTER 10

Within a few minutes, a policeman from Whitlow Junction had arrived and Charlie and I were being whisked off to Mount Holly, wherever that was.

"Excuse me, officer, but about what time do you think we'll arrive?" I asked, before taking a sip of coffee.

He quoted an hour's time. At least it wouldn't be too long of a trip.

"What's going on?" Charlie whispered nervously.

I quietly explained that I'd written a letter to a friend about our situation just in case things went wrong and that Ambrose had somehow gotten it to the addressee, who was trying to rescue us. I told him I didn't really know what was going on, but that we were probably in good hands, even if we might need to improvise a little.

Fortunately, the police officer wasn't chatty, preferring instead to scan the local country music stations.

Eventually, I saw the Mount Holly town sign and soon after, we pulled up to a small white clapboard house, neatly flanked by red rose bushes, where an elderly Black man and his wife stood waiting for us.

"Well, I'll be," said the surprised police officer. "*This* is your Cousin Dylan?"

"They're worth a fortune," I confided in low tones. "From the South African branch of the family," adding, "Very modest people."

After we'd said goodbye to the officer, we were greeted by the man.

"You're Dylan?" I asked.

"No, no," he said laughing. "My name's Henry. This is my wife, Vonetta."

I looked at Charlie, who probably looked as clueless as I did.

"I'm sorry, but who are you and why are we here?" I asked.

"My brother Ambrose contacted me. It's a long story. Please come inside," he said, welcoming us into the house.

"I just fixed breakfast," Vonetta said. "You boys must be hungry."

The smell of food was making my mouth water.

"Yes, we are," Charlie said. "We'd love some breakfast."

"Please, go on and sit yourselves down and I'll bring it right in," she said.

We didn't have to wait long before we each had a steaming plate of cheese grits, fried eggs, grilled ham steak, hot buttered biscuits, and fresh sliced tomatoes. I was famished.

As we ate, Henry explained that Ambrose had seen us being kidnapped and had called the bureau to speak with my friend Dylan.

I quickly looked over at Charlie when Henry said this, prepared to make an explanation about having friends in high places, but the news didn't seem to surprise him, which I thought was odd.

Henry went on to say that Dylan wanted to engineer a rescue for us but needed a place for us to stay temporarily, so Ambrose had offered Henry's house.

My head was swimming with a million questions.

"How did you know we'd be around here?" I asked.

"We didn't. That's where we had luck on our side," Henry said, smiling.

Vonetta came in to refill our coffee cups.

"Luck? Listen at him! It wasn't luck. I was up praying for you two all night," she asserted loudly.

Henry continued, "Dylan and Ambrose took a guess about how far from the train you might wind up, and it turned out to be pretty accurate."

"That's because the Lord was guiding their thoughts," Vonetta said over her shoulder on her way back to the kitchen.

"But someone came and freed us from the kidnappers. Do you know anything about that?" I asked. I didn't mention their having been murdered; no use involving Henry any more than he already was.

"Dylan said he would get you safe, but that he couldn't get too involved," Henry explained.

So that was it. Dylan knew there were things going on within the bureau and couldn't risk doing anything openly. The men who came to save them had probably been arranged in secret, most likely a personal favor Dylan requested rather than an official action by the bureau itself to save an agent in trouble.

At least now, I realized that there was definitely something wrong at the bureau and that Dylan was someone I could trust. However, Dylan was in danger too, so I couldn't count on his help for long.

After breakfast, Charlie was still feeling poorly so Henry suggested he lay on one of the couches in the sitting room and rest while Henry read the paper on the other. As Henry sat down, I could've sworn I saw the butt of a rifle between the couch cushions for just a second until he settled himself. He saw me noticing and gave me a pointed look. It was the same look Ambrose gave me when he told me about the train being stopped for a fuel-line issue that didn't exist.

Maybe Henry was keeping an eye on Charlie. Maybe there was something I didn't know about.

Meanwhile, I cleared the breakfast table and helped Vonetta wash the dishes.

"You don't need to do this," she said.

"No, really, I want to. I'm very grateful for your help and breakfast was absolutely delicious," I said.

"You look like you know your way around a sink," she said.

"I used to help my mother in the kitchen when I was little," I said. "And I work as a hair stylist."

"Do you really?" she said, smiling.

"I'm not sure how much Henry told you about my work, or how much Dylan told him," I said, "But I guess you could say I have two jobs. The everyday one is as a hair stylist."

"You married?" she asked.

"No," I said. "My other job is kind of dangerous. Most of my colleagues aren't married either."

Vonetta put down the dish she was drying and faced me squarely.

"I don't know what the future holds for you, son," she said, "But I will tell you that I will keep on praying for you, for the Lord to protect and guide you, and that someday, you'll find yourself a good husband."

I was startled by her remark; I suppose I assumed that she didn't know I was gay, or wouldn't approve because she was religious, or elderly, or any number of other ways I hadn't given her credit because of past experiences to the contrary.

She smiled at me.

"It's okay," she said sweetly. "My sister's boy, Curtis, was like you."

"Oh," I said. "Does he live in Mount Holly?"

"No. He went and moved to Oklahoma City years ago. But a group of boys up there, one night they got ahold of him, and they beat him to death."

CHAPTER 11

When the dishes were put away, I went into the sitting room to join Henry and the now-sleeping Charlie, but Henry rose quietly and motioned for me to come out into the back yard with him.

After following him out a distance from the house, he explained that Ambrose had figured out what was going on pretty quickly. Ambrose didn't know who I really was until he called Dylan, but he'd already suspected most of it.

I wondered why Henry was telling me this when he added something I didn't know and that hadn't been said earlier: each time I'd been out of the compartment to get food, Charlie had made calls to someone informing them of our location.

"What?" I asked. "How did Ambrose know that?"

"Old porter's trick," Henry said. "They put a drinking glass to the door and put their ear against it."

Apparently, Ambrose had gotten a strange vibe from Charlie and decided to check up on him while I was away.

At this point, I was so confused, I didn't know what was going on any more. All I knew was that I could trust Dylan and Ambrose. And at least now I had a much-needed secondary source of information, courtesy of Ambrose. Up to now, everything had been based on trusting whatever Charlie told me.

"If it isn't too much trouble, can I please use your phone? I've got to speak with Dylan," I said.

Henry said that I could.

"I have to tell you, I'm extremely grateful to you and Vonetta for your hospitality," I said. "With any luck, we'll be on our way soon. And I'm sorry you've been involved. I'd tell you more about the situation, but I'm afraid I can't."

"There's no need at all," Henry said, holding his hand with his palm towards me. "Dylan and I spoke at length about it and he explained the rules. I understand. I'm just happy to help."

Henry and I went back into the house and he told me there was a landline upstairs that I could use to contact Dylan. He said he'd keep an eye on Charlie, who was still sleeping.

As I ascended the steps, I thought of what I needed to tell him. It was a much shorter list than the things I needed to ask him.

When Dylan answered the phone, he sounded very relieved to hear from me.

"Thanks for coming through for me," I said.

"Don't thank me yet," he said. "I'm just finishing some arrangements for you. There's a place in Texarkana that has a car reserved under your name, and there's a bank just across the street—ask for a Mrs. Johnstone, she'll have money and a new ID for you." He told me the address and I scribbled it down.

"I can't talk long," he said.

"Dylan, I know something's going on there," I told him.

"Half the guys at the salon were trying to kill you and half weren't," he explained quickly. "There's a division here among the agents. They're being given orders to kill you on sight—some story about you selling critical government secrets and endangering our foreign agents—but not everyone's convinced it's true, so their aim isn't so good all of a sudden."

"Any idea who diverted the forensic work to my guy? He's on the murderer's payroll whoever he is," I explained.

"Don't know. I heard there's an internal—" he suddenly stopped and I heard him greet someone who'd entered his office.

"Look honey, I have to go. I'll pick up milk on the way home. Love you," he said as he hung up.

I sighed and looked at the receiver. Talking with Dylan was the first real sense of reassurance I'd had in days; someone at the bureau who was in my corner. The feeling of relief was immense.

Unfortunately, it didn't mean our difficulties were over. In fact, it meant there were plenty more, and I hadn't had the chance to figure out how long I'd have to keep all the plates in the air until the internal investigation Dylan began telling me about was done, or what further help I might be able to count on from Dylan. And I still knew nothing about Charlie's loyalties, since finding out he'd been feeding someone updates about our location.

When I got to the bottom of the stairs, Henry met me and asked if there were anything else he could do.

"I hate to ask, but can you drive us to Texarkana?" I said.

"Sure thing," he replied, nodding his head.

After waking Charlie and saying our goodbyes to Vonetta, we were off.

"The trip is over an hour, you might want to catch up on the news," Henry said, handing me his paper. I wasn't really interested in reading, but having a newspaper in front of my face gave me an excuse not to talk so I could think. However, my eye randomly caught a headline, one which tragically reminded me what all this mess was about: the serial killer had claimed another victim.

PART TWO

CHAPTER 12

The newspaper article offered few details, but the signature was the same as previous killings: the victim, a 21-year-old woman, had been eviscerated and strangled with her own intestines before being raped. The killer didn't just want his victims dead; he took his time—played with it—relishing the power he had over them. It was evident he took sadistic pleasure from it. His victims were all young, white, college-age women, and they all had one thing in common: they had rejected him in some way. He could not tolerate it. Had he not been a psychopath, he probably still would've been a spoiled and egotistical individual, capable of immense cruelty, but having the mind of a serial-killer escalated everything to horrific extremes, as evidenced by the gruesome story emblazoned on the front page of the newspaper in my hands.

So who was this boy? As I explained before, I'm not at liberty to say, but the general public even had a pretty good idea he was guilty, and law enforcement were absolutely convinced. He was the teenage son of a well-known Anglo-American dynastic family. They lived in Massachusetts and summered in Maine. They had homes in Palm Beach, Denver, and St. Moritz. Over the years, my own family had actually had glancing contact with them at certain charitable events of which we were mutual benefactors. It was from these encounters that we learned that the head of the family—the boy's father—was a particularly cold and ruthless individual. I'll be honest: families like mine aren't exactly overflowing with sugary sweetness, but this man was disdained by everyone. However, the enviable amount of power he wielded in high places kept everyone on good terms with him. *Au fond*, my people are a bunch of hypocrites, seriously, but even they had a hard time refraining from spitting after the mention of his name.

His children, a son and a daughter, were afforded advantages that even their aristocratic peers found breathtaking. Unsurprisingly, the daughter was involved in several rather flagrant scandals during college and quite a few shortly thereafter, but gradually faded into the background as her brother became the subject of intense gossip surrounding the murders.

The victims, all girls from well-to-do families, were either personal acquaintances of the boy, fellow students at the Ivy League university he attended, or had been seen by witnesses speaking with him. At first, those witnesses had been servants, valets, or caterers who reported on events they'd seen at parties, but eventually the continuation and the sheer brutality of the crimes encouraged the involvement of his cohorts and classmates. Had the victims been just any girls, these witnesses probably would've refrained from cooperating with police, knowing their social standing might suffer from the publicity, should they become embroiled in the investigation. However, in this case, they came willingly. The victims—whose bodies were found in several states, hence the involvement of the feds—were mostly girls from their own circle; girls who rode horses and played tennis and had coming-out parties. These high net-worth witnesses realized their own daughters and sisters could be next.

As for the boy's family, his mother had died of cancer some years previously and his father had taken up dalliances with shallow, fawning young women who were periodically dismissed and quickly replaced by other equally fawning and shallow young women. The father's parents (the boy's grandparents) were still alive and occupying a stately mansion in Maine, although the old gentleman was known to be in poor health and thus had handed the scepter to his son. Two famous and fabulously wealthy sisters were the boy's paternal aunts, each of whom had married into elite corporate families, and his two maternal uncles were a presidential cabinet appointee and a foreign ambassador, respectively.

Knowing a bit about human psychology, there was no doubt whatsoever in my mind that there must have been warning signs about the boy's twisted mental state, even in childhood. However, given the family's position in society, those signs would have been purposely ignored. It was tempting to think that the boy's parents had given him the benefit of the doubt in all cases because of their love for him, or perhaps because of their desire to protect him, but sadly, I knew all too well that the only love of which his father was capable was his love of self, and his only true protective desire that of his family's—and thus his own—reputation. The boy's father was a man who would go to any lengths, even murder, to keep justice from being served.

For local law enforcement and federal agencies, this created a thorny problem. In order to make an arrest, they had to have incontrovertible evidence that the boy did it. They simply stood to lose too much if they proceeded as they would with any average citizen because the boy was not an average citizen. He was the son of a family so powerful that a few phone calls could cost federal bureau chiefs to lose their jobs in disgrace and leverage lawsuits that could destroy local police forces. And they'd probably be facing all that even if they had sufficient circumstantial evidence and an eyewitness or two. But science was different.

Sure, things could be tampered with, but if several independent labs all came back with the same DNA results, no amount of tap-dancing on the part of any "expert testimony" of the defense's could convince a jury that the boy was innocent. With that, he could be convicted.

But first they had to find him, and Charlie was the only person who had a lead that might yield his whereabouts. The police and the feds probably didn't know about the existence of this shadowy branch of the family, this cousin and her kin. Maybe they had refused to play along with whatever was required to stay in the family's good graces, or possibly they'd balked at the strings attached to their inheritance and chosen to live relatively normal lives in the most out-of-the way place they could find: a tiny town in the remote Hill Country of America's second-largest state. In any event, I knew we would soon find out.

The news story about the murder made me realize how badly I wanted to see this boy—this monster—pay for what he had done. The coroners said the victims ultimately strangled to death, which meant the killer must have known what he was doing, and known how to do it very, very well. He would've had to cut their abdomens open carefully and disembowel them with the least possible loss of blood, which is difficult to do. This would ensure their consciousness during at least part of their strangulation, which would also not be a simple task, given the messy nature of slippery innards. More to the point, these murders weren't committed in a fit of rage or passion; they were done calmly and with care, which suggests to me—and to anyone with a shred of sense—that he knew *exactly* what he was doing, and he savored it.

In case you're wondering why I got into this business in the first place, and maybe thinking that I'm some kind of self-righteous punisher—that I'm not a compassionate individual, I can assure you that I am. I understand and accept that people make mistakes, sometimes egregious ones, and sometimes ones that cause others to lose their lives. They can get in bad situations and make painfully stupid choices. They can allow themselves to be controlled by negative emotions that drive them to do things of which they never imagined themselves capable. Add to that the possibility of an upbringing that included neglect or abuse, or a position low enough in society that makes them feel less-than on a continual basis and hopeless in the extreme, and they can do horrible things. I sincerely feel bad for these people and I have sympathy for their plight. In fact, in my role as a member of a prestigious family, I donate heartily to charities that try to help people like this so they never face a situation where they do something terrible because they don't feel there's any other way.

But I also believe there are those who are, quite simply, evil. They're like sharks, swimming constantly, unceasing in their quest for blood or wounded prey. With careful forethought and an utter absence of remorse, these individuals are creatures whose only joy, if it can be called that, is causing harm to others. Far from having tragic lives, they can hail from the most prosperous and loving of surroundings. They are adept at getting what they want by exploiting the honesty and kindness of others through charm and persuasiveness. They see everyone's weaknesses as clear as day, and use them to maximize their own advantage. And if anyone stands in their way, they hate them with an unimaginable fury.

I do what I do because that fury doesn't scare me.

Maybe that makes me crazy, or maybe it means I believe in something stronger that's inside me; probably a combination of both, and don't ask me to explain it because I can't. It's just something I know. But that's why instead of living off my trust fund and pretending to care about polo matches, I found myself sitting in Henry's car with Charlie, headed for Texarkana, on our way south to find a serial killer's cousin.

"Seen anything that interested you?" asked Henry, taking back his paper.

"Nothing I haven't seen before," I replied bitterly.

CHAPTER 13

When we got to Texarkana, Henry pulled up to the bank. I thanked him and then Charlie and I went inside. Sure enough, the envelope containing money and a new ID for me were there, just as Dylan promised, and then Charlie and I crossed the street to the place where our rental car was waiting. The first thing I did, after making up a story about how a good friend was able to arrange everything for me, was to drive us to a fast-food restaurant where we spent a lot of time in the restroom getting ourselves cleaned up. I still had dust on my face and Charlie's hair, which was very fine and apt to tangling, was all over the place. I didn't have a comb, but I was able to wet it down and make it look presentable. My own hair was conveniently coarse enough that it stayed in place mostly, but I definitely needed a shave. Then again, trends being what they were, I could pass as being stylish, not sloppy, as long as I dressed well.

Our clothes definitely looked like a mess after rough traveling and a night in the woods, so our next stop was a local merchant that sold basics, you know—cowboy kind of stuff: button-down shirts, jeans, and boots. That's normally not my thing, but it occurred to me that we should blend in where we were headed, so that's what we bought and wore out of the store, putting our other clothes in the shopping bag. I don't think the outfit did much for me, but Charlie actually looked better in the stiff Western-style shirt than he did in his usual polo shirt, which showed off his paunch too obviously. There was something that bothered me a lot, though. I caught sight of his back briefly while we were changing into our new clothes in the fitting room at the store. It looked like there were red welts all over it, not new ones, but ones that resulted from blows given a long time ago that had never healed. I decided to say nothing, at least at the moment.

We started for Fredericksburg, which was a nine-hour drive. I marveled at the grand scale of the southwestern states; nine hours was barely enough to get from one outpost of civilization to another. Charlie seemed to be feeling a little better, and while he didn't look like he was in pain any more, I could tell he was becoming apprehensive.

"Nervous about finding that woman?" I asked.

He hesitated a moment before answering, "Yes."

"Have you got any idea where she might live?" I inquired.

"Some little road off Milam Street," he said. "A couple miles from town."

"Look, there's nothing to worry about," I said. "You know your stuff; it's probably the right woman. We'll go and explain that you tracked down her DNA connection to the killer and ask if she knows where he's hiding. For God's sake, she might actually have him staying there and be willing to give him up after the discovery of his latest victim. I mean, if she has any sympathy at all, she'll do the right thing."

I told Charlie about what I'd read in the paper, and how the situation might work to our advantage if the killer's cousin could be convinced that any information she could give us about where he might be hiding could save a life. Somehow, though, Charlie seemed distant. Maybe he wasn't feeling as well as I thought.

I remembered the marks on his back.

"There's something bothering me that I need to ask you about," I said.

Charlie looked very apprehensive.

"When we were changing in that fitting room, I couldn't help noticing that you have some welts on your back. Is that from something that happened when you were a child?" I asked.

"Oh that," Charlie said dismissively. "I forget they're there because I can't see them. Yeah, that's from when I was a kid. I told you my father was a criminal. He also wasn't always in a good mood."

I was grateful for his honesty, but something about it still troubled me deeply.

"Listen, I know in those days a lot of kids got hit, especially boys, but even from what little I could see, those marks . . ." I could hardly finish my sentence, but what I was thinking was: *those marks are the result of a savage beating.*

"If it's all the same to you," Charlie said, becoming agitated, "can we not talk about this any more?"

"Sure; that's fine," I said quickly. "And I'm sorry if I . . ."

"Never mind, okay? Just never mind," he said. He shook his head and looked out the window. Then he said, "You really don't know when to shut up."

I couldn't believe what I'd heard. I was instantly infuriated.

"Excuse me?" I demanded. "You're telling me I don't know when to shut up? I, who rescued you from the feds and a band of hired killers, got you across the country, kept you alive in the woods, and got us back on track again?"

"Just forget it," he mumbled.

"No," I snapped, the strain and exhaustion of the past few days finally revealing their toll on my mood. "No, I don't think I will," I continued, adding, "as a matter of fact, I have another question for you: who the hell were you talking to when I left our train compartment?"

"What do you mean?" he asked blankly.

"You were telling someone our location. Who? Who was it?" I asked.

"Where did you get that idea?" he asked.

“Who was it?” I persisted, remembering as I did so that interrogation was not my strong suit.

“This—this woman I’ve been seeing,” he said unconvincingly. “I told her I was going to visit a sick relative as an excuse for cancelling some plans we had this weekend. That’s all.”

I knew Charlie was lying through his teeth, but I realized I wasn’t going to get him to talk, at least not this way.

“Oh,” I said, matter-of-factly, my anger fading. “I guess that’s what it was then. I’m sorry I doubted you.”

We rode in uncomfortable silence for a couple of minutes. When I couldn’t stand it anymore, I took a deep breath.

“Charlie, I promise I’m not going to talk about your back again, but I’d like to talk about why I asked,” I began. He seemed to be listening. “When you’re a hair stylist, people tell you a lot of things, and you’re my only client that doesn’t really open up. I mean, sure, you tell me about your work and all, but you don’t say much about yourself. I sort of formed the impression that you were an introverted kind of guy, but more than that, you were sort of sad, or depressed, or feeling bad about yourself. Then I come to find out about your father. I can’t even imagine what you went through growing up with that, and then finding the strength to get away from it. I honestly can’t.” My voice was starting to break unexpectedly as emotions arose in me, but I continued. “And I have a feeling he did more than beat you. He tore you apart on the inside. And you want to know why I know? Because that happened to me too.” I glanced at Charlie and his eyes were full of pain, but he said nothing. “We have something in common. Instead of being told that we were good, worthy, and deserving, we were told we were worthless and deficient. We weren’t worthy of our father’s attention. They dismissed us. And what happened to us? We not only hurt from the pain they inflicted upon us, but we formed *ideas* because of it. We formed ideas about *who we are* and we formed the idea that we are the kind of people that deserved to be abused that way.” I stopped for a moment to wipe the back of my hand across my eyes because my tears were blinding me and I couldn’t see the road. When I finally composed myself, I finished. “Until the day we die, Charlie, we’ll carry those scars inside us. And whatever worthwhile things we do with our lives, some part of us will always feel that we have nothing to offer.”

There was another long silence, but this time, it was because we were reeling from the remembrance of having been denied the one thing we needed most from our fathers: their approval. We both knew it. Charlie didn’t say a word for the remainder of the trip, but I knew I’d touched a nerve.

A couple of times during the next few hours, I thought I saw cars that looked suspicious overtaking us, but then they drove on past, and I realized I was being paranoid. Probably just another symptom of the strain I was under.

We got dinner at a drive-in and ate while we drove, which I normally hate to do, but I wanted to get to Fredericksburg as quickly as we could. The cousin might already have been killed. I hoped there was cellphone reception at her house so I could call the local police if necessary.

By the time we got into town and were driving down Main Street, I could understand why the killer's cousin had chosen this place. It really was in the middle of nowhere. However, I could see all kinds of giant striped tents pitched on what appeared to be a commons area.

"I wonder what that's for," I said aloud.

"For Oktoberfest," Charlie answered. "They have it every year. It's a town that was settled by Germans and they keep the old traditions."

Seemed like he knew a lot about a hole-in-the-wall town we were only at to find a relative of the killer. "How'd you know all that?" I asked.

"Oh," he said lightly, "I read about it when I was looking up the town."

We turned up Milam Street and headed north towards the cousin's house. Several miles later, Charlie indicated I should pull off on a small side road, which I did.

"It's down here," he said, indicating one of the ranches whose gates we were approaching. He got out of the car and opened the gate allowing me to drive through. Then he closed the gate behind us and got back in the car. The long driveway was covered in loose clay so yellow I could see it even in the dark. It rose in choking clouds behind us. It must have been a dry autumn, but then again, it was probably always dry in these parts.

We finally got to a small brick house and I parked the car, getting out and peering around me in the darkness after I'd turned off the car's headlights. It was a moonless night and I couldn't see anything. I heard Charlie get out of the car but somehow, he was gone when I turned to look for him. I started towards the front door, and that's the last thing I remember.

CHAPTER 14

Waking up took a while. I was vaguely conscious for a little bit, then felt pain and probably fell back into unconsciousness again for a long time. Finally, I awoke fully, acutely aware of intense heat. I was lying on the ground in some kind of shed and I could see bright daylight through the cracks; it was probably noon, and it was sweltering. The heat compounded the blinding pain in my head. I thought to myself that this had been the second time in just a few days that I'd been knocked unconscious, and it probably wasn't a good thing to take up on a regular basis. I had a newfound respect for prizefighters.

When I tried to move, I found my hands were tightly tied behind me, as were my feet. They hadn't taped my mouth, which told me that I was somewhere remote enough that nobody would care if I yelled, which meant I was probably still at the ranch where we arrived at the previous night.

I lay there for a long time, trying to summon the will to figure things out. My thoughts were swimming and I was oddly calm, considering I knew I was in danger. Or perhaps I had become discouraged by the mental and physical fatigue of the past few days and had given up completely.

"You're a quitter; you'll always be a quitter," I could hear my father saying. Maybe he was right. I dozed again for a little bit as I contemplated my failure, but the oppressive heat wouldn't let me rest. I was miserable.

Is this really how I want it to end? I asked myself. Then I thought of Charlie. I was an agent of the United States government, and I had sworn to protect the people of my country. If I gave up now and let myself be overtaken by whoever had tied such remarkably tight knots around my limbs, I'd be shirking my duty.

There's one thing you learn when you come from a prominent family, at least a good one with a long heritage of wealth and power, and that's that you have a duty to others. You have a reputation to uphold that may go back several generations. You can't afford to let the team down.

Surprisingly bolstered by the memory of ancestors who'd braved all manner of hardships and adversity to make their mark on the world and better their situation for the benefit of posterity, I sat up. I winced in pain the moment I was upright, but I called to mind the portraits hanging above the stairway in the house in which I grew up. The faces were composed of the same flesh and bones in mine, and their expressions all but screamed, "Don't you *dare* let them break you."

I had a duty to fulfill. I had to find Charlie and rescue him from whatever fate had befallen him.

I slid myself to one side of the shed and peered out through the cracks. The shed I was sitting in was situated about 15 yards from the brick ranch house we'd arrived at last night. I could see the car still out front. It would be useless for me to kick open the shed door because I couldn't escape on foot being tied as I was. Believe it or not, most people—even professional criminals—don't know how to tie good knots, but whoever tied these did a first-class job.

Just then, I heard a screen door slam shut and Charlie came out of the house with a bottle of water. I couldn't believe my eyes. He was free.

He unlocked the padlock on the shed and opened the door.

"How're you feeling?" he asked, squatting down next to me and opening the bottle of water.

The sunlight streamed in and blinded me, but I still couldn't believe my eyes.

Before I could say anything, Charlie explained, "It was me who hit you last night. Sorry. I had to."

He gave me a drink of water, which I desperately needed. I decided not to ask any questions so I could consume as much water as possible. Especially in this part of the country, water was critical.

"Who the hell tied these knots?" I asked, as soon as I had finished drinking.

"I did," Charlie said. "I had to tie you good since I knew you were a fed."

"How'd you know?" I asked him.

"Because I'm a fed, too."

I was incredulous. Nothing made sense. I'd spent the last several days dragging a federal agent across the country to save his life, and now he was holding me captive for reasons beyond my comprehension.

Charlie laughed a little. "Yeah. If it had been up to me, back in the woods in Arkansas, we would've been hunting berries instead of eating those damn rotten acorns, but I couldn't let on that I knew how to forage better than you."

"But how—" I began, starting to ask a question I didn't even know how to ask.

Charlie interrupted me. "Haven't been a fed for a long time. That's how I got so out of shape," he said, indicating his torso. "I was only in it a few years. It wasn't for me."

"What the hell is going on?" I asked. "Where's the murderer's cousin? Is she here?"

"There's no cousin," he said. "This is my pa's place."

"So why are we here?" I asked.

"Well," Charlie began, "*I'm* here because I needed to get away from the feds, and I was able to get you to help me. Here's where I grew up."

With sudden clarity, I understood why so many things hadn't made sense: the questions Charlie never asked that any average person would surely have asked . . . the odd behaviors that couldn't be explained away . . . something else, a much bigger situation, had been at work the entire time. My best bet was to reason with Charlie.

"Look, whatever went wrong, I can help you. I can talk to the feds. Hiding out here at your father's ranch isn't going to solve anything. They'll find you eventually. If you just let me help, I can negotiate on your behalf. I have connections," I assured him.

Charlie shook his head. "You know, for an otherwise likeable guy, the one thing about you that annoys the hell out of me is how you always think you know everything," he said.

"What?" I asked plaintively. "What don't I know?"

"My father's in a crime ring associated with the syndicate," he replied. "They were the ones who helped us escape from the salon. They were going to pull you off the train and shoot you and bring me to Texas, but your friend at headquarters intervened and sent some feds to knock them off. That really threw me off schedule."

So Ambrose and Henry had had good reason to doubt Charlie; they knew he wasn't as innocent as he looked.

"Then this is about a lot more than you trying to get away from whoever hired you to do genealogical research," I concluded.

"It's about showing my father that I'm somebody now, and that I can help with the family business, so to speak," he explained. "At this point, since you're still around, you've become a convenient hostage. Never know when we might need one."

"I can't believe this is the road you're going down," I told him, and I meant it. "You told me what your father was, and how hard you worked to get away from that life. Whatever money or things you acquire, they won't be worth anything—believe me, I'm speaking from personal experience."

"Yes, I know; you're a little rich boy. I found out all about you. But that's not why I'm doing it. It's time I show my father he can be proud of me," he said.

"You'll never be able to convince him of that because he doesn't love you and he doesn't care about you. Can't you see that? Maybe it's easy to forget about those scars because they're on your back, but some part of you must realize that he wrote you off a long time ago. Being a criminal is nothing to be proud of. Save yourself before it's too late. I swear I'll help you. It's my duty," I exclaimed, adding, "You know that."

I saw a pained look quickly play across Charlie's face before he turned to leave the shed, saying, "I'll be back later with more water."

CHAPTER 15

At the very least, finally, I felt like I understood what was going on. There was some comfort in that.

I also realized that I had only myself—and my own ego—to blame for having thought I was so clever; Charlie had hit the nail on the head with that one. I thought I was so much brighter than he was, and here I didn't even have a clue what was going on all around me.

It was a harsh reminder that I was largely responsible for the position in which I found myself.

Speaking of, I realized with anguish that my chances of survival were not good. I wouldn't be able to escape, and it was only a matter of time before they killed me. Even if Charlie didn't want to (and I had no idea what his feelings on the subject might be), it would be the only option. Keeping me alive as a witness would be too dangerous.

As for keeping me as a hostage, I reckoned that was just something Charlie said. In truth, I would be of little value to them. If the feds found them, they would come down hard on them, hostage or no hostage. Too much was at stake to make concessions to spare the life of one agent. With a deep sigh, I acknowledged to myself it didn't work that way.

Barring an unforeseen miracle, I was done for.

Still, I had to keep my head about me in the unlikely event an opportunity of some kind presented itself.

First, I had to get things straight in my head (which had become slightly less painful) about what exactly was going on. Charlie was involved with his father, who was involved with a crime syndicate. He needed to escape the feds, which I unwittingly helped him do, and the syndicate helped us get away—they were the ones driving the bus at the salon, the one which crashed into the feds' vehicle blocking our path out of the driveway. Little by little the loose ends were tied up. When we were on the train, Charlie had been calling his father to relay our location, and the four bruisers that got on the train and removed us—the ones I thought behaved like professional hitmen—*were* professional hitmen. I was afraid they were going to kill us, but they were there to rescue Charlie and take him to Texas. I was supposed to end up face down in the forest in Arkansas with a bullet in my head, but Dylan's intervention starring of a couple of federal agents ended those plans. Ambrose and Henry suspected Charlie was up to no good and treated him accordingly, while I was revealing myself to him incrementally, although it wouldn't have made a difference anyway, since he already knew I was a fed. And Charlie had led me down to Texas under the pretext of finding the murderer's nonexistent cousin when in actuality, he was just coming home to reunite with his father's gang.

I thought for a moment. That was a lot to process in my weakened condition.

However, some things still didn't make sense. What was the genealogy assignment all about? Was that real? *Had* the feds contacted Charlie to match crime-scene DNA to potential relatives of the murderer? If so, why were they after him? He must have done something to justify their pursuit of him, and judging by their ferocity, it must have been pretty bad.

I thought back to the day Charlie had begged for help. His fear was genuine, I knew that. They were on to him for something, I just didn't know what.

Meanwhile, what had brought Charlie to me? Was it a coincidence that I, his hair stylist, just happened to be a fed in deep cover? Did he find out after he'd already started coming to me for haircuts, or did he choose me because he knew who I was?

Things still weren't completely adding up.

Charlie was definitely right—there was plenty I didn't know.

CHAPTER 16

The rest of that day passed with me languishing in the heat inside the shed. A man I assumed to be a member of Charlie's father's gang came out in the early evening and put a bowl of chili down for me. I was starving, so I unceremoniously ate it by putting my face into it like a dog.

Afterwards, I tried wiping my face clean on the interior wall of the shed when through the cracks, I saw a man who turned out to be Charlie's father coming out of the house. Charlie came out after him.

"But Pa," he protested, "Let me come with you tonight."

"I said no," the man asserted coldly.

I squinted and took a good look at him. He was old, but the kind of man who still had a certain charisma about him. Despite his age, he was muscular and fit. He must've been pretty fierce back in the day, I thought. He was still good-looking, with rugged features and snow-white hair, slicked back at the sides like they did in the 1950s. His heyday had been in the time of the pompadour, clearly.

I marveled at the fact that this attractive man was the father of Charlie, who, by comparison, was such a nondescript lump of a guy. Then I remembered something Charlie himself had told me: that people have more of their mother's genes than their father's. I began to see what had happened. Charlie's father was probably a sociopath—a charming, handsome sociopath—and he'd chosen a plain woman as his wife, knowing she'd always feel she didn't deserve him and would allow herself to be treated poorly just to be with him. That's how it worked.

"Pa, look, I can help you—just give me a chance," Charlie was saying.

His father turned on him, his blue eyes shining with fury. "I don't need no help from you. Get your fat ass back in that house." Then he got into a truck and slammed the door.

A cloud of yellow dust and pebbles shot up in the wake of his back tires as he drove off, leaving Charlie staring after him in disappointment. He stayed like that for a moment or two before going back into the house.

I lay down again on the floor of the shed, since sitting up was uncomfortable due to the way I was tied, but a minute later, I heard the screen door slam and saw Charlie coming. He had a bottle of water.

Once inside the shed, he offered to take me to the bathroom. Having had little to drink and hardly anything to eat, I didn't actually have to go, but I said I did, thinking any chance to get out of the shed brought me one step closer to freedom, and that freedom could only come from Charlie. I had to talk sense into him.

He untied my feet. I could barely stand from the cramping in my legs, but I managed, and he led me out of the shed. I started towards the house, but he pulled me back.

"No," he said. "You can't use the toilet in the house. Out here in the brush," he said, pointing to a clump of scraggly trees nearby.

I followed where he led me, and I said, "So things aren't going as well as you thought."

"Just shut up," he snapped. I'd never heard him so mad.

"I'm not trying to be facetious—honestly, I'm not. What I mean is that things aren't happening the way you hoped they would, and I can tell you why. It's because he doesn't love you," I said, adding, "That'll never change."

"You don't know anything," he stated, raising his voice.

"Trust me on this, if only because it's like that with me and my father, too. He never came around. Never. He's disgusted with me, and the look on his face when he talks to me is exactly like the look on your old man's face when he talks to you." I paused. "For God's sake, listen to me; I'm trying to help you."

"I can't do this anymore," hissed Charlie, stopping in his tracks and putting his head in his hands. He started to cry.

"You don't have to do this anymore," I assured him. "It's over any time you say it is. There's a way out."

Charlie stood there covering his eyes with his hands and I watched his shoulders heaving as his frame shook with grief. He'd endured a lifetime of abuse at the hands of his father, made a daring attempt to be appreciated, and failed. He was a broken man, and I was watching him fall to pieces.

I gave him a moment because I knew he was experiencing something very intense. When I did speak, I said, "I know you're better than that."

He looked up at me with swollen eyes.

"You know how it is; we're trained to judge people's character. I'll tell you something—Ambrose and Henry? They pegged you for a criminal, but not me. I swear it. That's because I saw something else. You're a man who hates the sight of his own reflection. You know what? So am I."

Luckily for me, he was listening. I went on.

"The two of us, we made new lives for ourselves. I know how much courage it took you to leave the family because I did it too. And I understand why you thought you could come back and things would be different. That's the problem with both of us: we think someday, somehow, we'll be good enough, but it'll never happen," I said. "It isn't about what *we* lack, it's about what *they* lack; they don't have it in them to care about us."

At this point, Charlie was just standing there with his head down.

"Please, untie me," I said. "We've got the car, we can get out of here."

"What'll happen?" Charlie asked.

"You know what'll happen. You'll spend some time in jail, but not as much as if you keep going. I'll call my contact at the bureau as soon as we get out of here and I promise I'll do everything I can for you. We can make this work," I said.

In case you're wondering, I meant every word I said. I wasn't just playing for time or the chance to get away. I understood why Charlie had done what he did, and I had a lot of sympathy for him. As I'd told him, we had a lot in common. I couldn't count the times I'd gone home to my father, hoping for even a shred of compassion or acceptance, and then wondering what utter insanity ever made me think it could be possible. It was like going after a mirage of water in the desert and ending up with a mouthful of sand. And yet I did it again and again, just like Charlie.

I sighed aloud and looked Charlie in the eye. "Are we going to do this?" I asked.

"Yeah," he said, taking a pocket-knife from his jeans and cutting my hands free. I could barely control them, numb as they were, the nerves having been compressed for so long by the tightness of the rope, but I shook them out as we walked back towards the car.

"Get the keys and some money; I'll wait in the shed until you come out, and then start up the car and I'll jump in before you take off," I instructed.

Charlie went into the house while I concealed myself back in the shed. A moment later he reappeared. When I heard the ignition, I ducked down and sprinted to the car, getting in quickly. We drove down the long driveway, away from the ranch house, until we got to the gate.

"Open it," Charlie said.

Hoping no one in the house would see me, I got out and opened the gate. Charlie pulled through and I was about to get back in the car but Charlie told me to close it, lest it look suspicious. Nobody ever left the gate open.

I got out of the car again and just as I was heading for the gate, I saw two men standing in front of the house pointing at me. We'd been discovered. I dashed back into the car and slammed the door, telling Charlie to take off.

The road into Fredericksburg was long, but Charlie knew it like the back of his hand, and he drove quickly. I was grateful Charlie was driving because I was so exhausted from my ordeal that I could hardly hold my head up, but I knew I'd have to pull myself together to face what lie ahead.

"Give me your phone," I said. "I'm going to try calling my contact if I can get reception."

"It's spotty but you should be able to," he said, handing it to me. I realized at that moment that we weren't as we'd been the first time we'd traveled together, with me, a government agent, protecting him, a civilian. Now we were equals. It was good.

As I dialed Dylan, I heard Charlie say, "Uh-oh."

Looking in the side mirror, I could see a speck of a car way in the distance behind us. They were far off, but it wouldn't be long before they caught us unless Charlie could outrun them.

My thoughts were interrupted when I heard someone say "Hello?" on the other end.

"Dylan!" I exclaimed.

"I'm sorry," said the unfamiliar voice. "Who are you trying to reach?"

I held the phone away from my head. I thought of asking for my supervisor, but no telling whose side he was on. Clearly, Dylan was gone. I hoped he wasn't dead. This was getting too complicated for me. Realizing it was going to be a lot harder to get help than I thought, I hung up.

"What's the matter?" asked Charlie. I explained. He wasn't happy about it.

"We can always get the local cops to help us," I said.

"Against the crowd that's after us? That's not very reassuring," he said.

"You have a better idea?" I asked. The speck of a car was now twice the previous size.

CHAPTER 17

By the time we rolled into town a few minutes later, our pursuers were almost upon us. Charlie had deftly taken a few side-street turns once we reached the residential area off the main street, but going as slow as we had to, they'd be on us in no time.

Glancing down one of the small avenues, I was startled to see a familiar face: Dylan's. He was getting into a car half a block away.

"Stop!" I shouted to Charlie. "Turn around and head down there!" I said, pointing towards Dylan. "That's my contact!"

Charlie wheeled the car around and we made it down the street just out of sight of the car chasing us, which I saw continue past in the side-view mirror, although a moment later I heard brakes screeching, so they'd realized we'd turned off. We'd have to be quick.

"Pull over," I indicated, and Charlie and I jumped out.

"Dylan!" I shouted, "It's me! Help us!"

Dylan hit the unlock button and we dove into his car. He took off and rounded the corner just as the car following us came down the block. They would think we were in our car, and by the time they figured out otherwise, we would be off with Dylan.

"Where should I go?" Dylan asked.

"If you go three streets and make a right, there's a grocery store on your left. Pull in and go around to the parking lot in the back. I used to work there as a kid," said Charlie.

Charlie and I kept our heads down until Dylan arrived in the back lot.

"Any sign of the guys chasing us?" I asked Dylan.

"I didn't see anyone, but we have to be careful. I'm here on my own," he explained.

Before I could tell him what was going on, Dylan pulled his gun and aimed it at Charlie.

"He's not who you think he is," Dylan told me. "He works for the syndicate."

"I know all about that," I said. "His father's crime ring is involved with them. Put the gun away; he's through with them. He wants to come clear."

"He's got a lot more blood on his hands than you think," Dylan said, still holding Charlie at gunpoint. I turned to Charlie.

I was about to ask him what Dylan meant by this, but at that moment, Charlie flung the door open and ran from the car. He ducked around the corner of the grocery store. Dylan and I followed on foot, but it was too late. The men in the other car, who'd been circling the area where they'd last seen us, spotted him out front and picked him up. In a flash, he was gone.

"They're heading for Main Street," Dylan said, as he drove out of the parking lot.

"What's going on?" I asked. "What are you doing here?"

"They sent me down to get set up—twenty more agents will be here within the hour," he answered.

"*Twenty?*" I asked, incredulously. That was a lot; they'd only send that many for something on a grand scale.

He went on to relate that the case of the murderer had taken a turn that brought it to this area. The boy's family owned an enormous ranch in the neighboring town of Kerrville. His family, hoping to distance him from the most recent murder, and probably hoping to keep him somewhere remote enough that he wouldn't kill again, had sent him down the day before.

The part that was most upsetting to learn was that Charlie's father's gang was directly connected with the syndicate members who worked for the murderer's family.

"How much involvement are we talking?" I asked.

Dylan explained that Charlie's father had been helpful to them on several occasions and was taking payments from the murderer's family via the mob.

"Wait a minute," I said, as Dylan stopped for a red light. "I get the part about Charlie working with his father's gang, who are involved with the syndicate—but what does any of this have to do with the murders?"

Dylan told me the murderer's family had a lot of holdings in Texas, most of them under different names, and Charlie's father's gang were instrumental in helping coordinate things for them.

Having seen Charlie's father, I couldn't imagine him showing up in board rooms and leveraging powerful networking connections.

When I said so, Dylan explained, "No, it's nothing that sophisticated. We're talking physical threats and intimidation, mysterious fires, that kind of thing. Just the other day, they took out one of the staff at the ranch in Kerrville who heard the son was coming to stay. We found her body this morning, or at least what was left of it."

The light turned green and Dylan drove on. I was beginning to understand this was a much bigger tangle of evil than I'd previously thought.

"The internal investigation uncovered someone at the top who was paid off by the mob. They're still sorting things out, but everything is mostly cleared up." He paused a moment. "I resigned," he added.

"Why?" I asked, shocked by what he said. He was an outstanding agent.

"Got my kids to think about. Claudia's nearly two and she's hardly ever seen me," he quipped.

Claudia was his baby daughter; I'd seen photos of her and Dylan's son in his office. They were adorable.

"After this, I'm done," he said.

Darkness was falling but the town was brightly lit for the Oktoberfest celebration. Parked cars were everywhere, people spilling out onto the street and walking several blocks to get to the tents. I could hear the faint strains of music.

"What do we do now?" I asked.

"If we can locate Charlie and his father—keep an eye on them until the others get here—we can take them in," he replied.

As I watched the happy people walking past us on their way to the festival, I felt bad that Charlie was back on the wrong side of the law, but it had been his choice, and he'd bolted.

That reminded me of something I needed to ask Dylan: "What did Charlie have to do with me in the first place?"

Dylan turned to look at me as he stopped for the next red light. "You don't know?" he asked with a look of surprise.

"No," I said.

"When Charlie came to the salon," he began, but then I saw him glance into the rear-view mirror, where something caught his eye. It was only a fraction of a second, but I saw an expression on his face that made me brace myself by grabbing the door-handle.

A shot blasted through the window, and broken glass and Dylan's blood were everywhere. Someone ran past the car. I should've given chase, but I heard Dylan gasping desperately, trying to say something. Blood was pouring from his mouth and neck. Within seconds, I knew he would be dead.

"Clau—, Claud—," he sputtered.

"I know—Claudia. I'll tell her all about you. I'll take care of them," I promised.

Dylan's head fell back and he was lifeless. I hoped he'd heard me honor his dying wish.

I knew I had to get out of there; whoever killed Dylan would be coming for me next. That's when I felt a strange stinging sensation in my right shoulder—they'd hit me too. I'd been so startled by Dylan's murder that I didn't even know I'd been shot. The first round must have disoriented me. No telling how many shots he'd fired. Maybe he thought we were both dead. I could only hope so.

CHAPTER 18

Upon exiting the car, I discovered I'd also been grazed by a bullet in the leg; fortunately, it just missed the knee. I could walk. I'd never been shot at before, never saw anyone die right in front of me. Given my physical and emotional state, it was no wonder it wasn't registering properly. The mind does curious things to protect itself.

It was clear the body did, as well. I was in shock, I knew, so I might as well make the most of it and keep moving before everything hit me, while I still had the benefit of adrenaline coursing through my system in quantities it had never known. They told us in training that we were built to survive, and at that moment, I knew it was true.

They also told us humans were predators, the deadliest on the planet, to be exact. My thoughts focused on the murderer, how he was attended by death everywhere he went. Either he was killing, or others were killing to protect him. It was ironic. Who was there to protect everyone else from him?

I am, I heard myself say aloud.

A wave of dizziness hit me and I swayed for a moment before regaining my footing. People were screaming and staring at me. Using my shirt collar, I wiped Dylan's blood from my face. I started to walk, then I ran.

I could hear sirens. The cops couldn't protect me from what was after me. I didn't know what to do next, except that I had to keep moving. Somewhere in the back of my mind, an instructor had said that humans have the unfortunate habit of holding still when danger strikes, presumably to figure out what's going on, but that it was the worst reaction. I had to move. Moving meant life.

After going a block towards the main street, I cut into the crowd. There were so many people, Dylan's shooting had only been a fringe incident. The sound of the music and singing drowned it out and only those right next to it reacted.

As I pressed through the crowd, working my way inwards, I realized I was perspiring and disheveled, but so was everyone else. The blood was the only giveaway that something was wrong. At that moment, I saw a public rest room and darted in. As I stood at the sink washing blood off my face and hands and creating a makeshift bandage with paper towels for my shoulder (which, fortunately, had only been grazed after all), a tough young cowboy came in and, seeing my appearance, asked, "What in the hell happened to you?"

"Nothin'," I replied. "Just got myself into a fight."

"At's it, boy," he laughed loudly, unzipping his fly. "You give 'em hell!"

When I left the bathroom, it occurred to me that Texas was one of the few places where being beaten and bloody didn't really make you any the worse off in the eyes of strangers.

I'd had several gulps of blessedly cold water from the sink, which I hoped would sustain me until . . . the thought went unfinished in my mind, as I couldn't think that far ahead.

All I could retain was that the other feds would be there within a few hours. Dylan had said so. Also, Charlie and his father and their gang were at the festival, although I didn't know why.

I began walking through the crowd, looking for anything that would point me in the right direction. There were beer tents everywhere, and vendors selling grilled German sausages and smoked turkey legs. Two little girls giggled as they passed in front of me carrying an immense fried funnel-cake, covered in a hapless storm of powdered sugar. Further away, there were tents for dancing. Someone was yodeling. A few passers-by wore dirndl skirts or lederhosen. Others carried souvenirs, such as ceramic beer steins or imported handmade crafts.

I didn't have a reliable sense of time, but as it grew darker, I figured it had been about 20 minutes since the shooting. The police would be on scene, and witnesses would be telling them that I was in the car. They'd be looking for me. They wouldn't cancel the event because it was too big—not only was it obviously the town's primary money-maker, but the cops couldn't stop it if they wanted to; the crowd was enormous. It would take a bomb blast to scatter them.

I continued walking in the direction away from the shooting, when I heard a woman shrieking.

"Get your hands off me," I could hear her saying. Instinctively, I turned and saw a pretty blonde grappling with a man who looked somehow out of place. He had neatly trimmed hair and was wearing a crisp white long-sleeved polo shirt, impeccably pressed chino pants, a classic leather belt, and boat shoes. It was a New England look. A wealthy New England look.

I pressed forwards towards him, but not before a couple of older men exchanged words with him. I couldn't hear what was said, but someone gave him a powerful shove and he almost fell over into a tent where a vendor was selling Bowie knives and paperweights with scorpions in them. The girl was escorted away by some friends.

Coming closer, I saw the young man put his hand on his chest in the place where they'd shoved him. I saw him smart; it must have hurt. A couple of the paperweights had been knocked off the vendor's table in the scuffle. The vendor cried out, "Hey," to the young man.

"Fuck you," he said casually, walking off.

Surer than anything I'd ever known, I knew that was the murderer.

He was a psychopath. People were like things to him, to be grabbed or scattered at will. The innocent would assume he could change, projecting their own sensibilities on him, as people invariably do, but they would be wrong—dead wrong. He was a ghoul dressed in human flesh. Born without a conscience or care for anything other than his own wants, he'd developed into the most grotesque monstrosity possible by being denied genuine love and caring during childhood. He was the result of a perfect storm of familial failure and psychological derangement. He would never stop killing because it amused him. Seeing his altercation with the young woman, I saw his M.O.: he'd approach someone whom he found attractive, but his come-on would be too strong; it would be socially inappropriate. The young woman would understandably balk, and that's when he would get rough, convincing himself that she deserved to be hurt for turning him down. His status and power meant he could force those women to come with him, generally without interference from anyone, except here. Nobody in Texas knew him. While his family owned a massive ranch, they weren't resident and so his name carried no weight. Even if people recognized it, the Texas social world was a thing unto itself. Millionaires as myopic and tacky as you could imagine became self-appointed guardians of the gates, and their cliquishness ensured nobody got in. They were oblivious to the fact that East Coast socialites would laugh in their faces at the very thought of them calling themselves "elite," but they were what they were, and they didn't care. They held their ridiculous traditional fetes and enjoyed exclusive memberships at private venues where they and other racist snobs collectively held court, waving the flag and taking pride in their "values." It was a great big "good ol' boys'" club, and this young man, Harvard-educated, descended from Mayflower passengers, with the blood of medieval English nobles coursing through his veins, was a nothing.

For his part, the boy probably didn't realize there were parts of the world where his name wouldn't move mountains. He was sheltered, traveling from international hotspot to international hotspot, places where his family was revered, and only frequenting those parts of America where the nation's social scions ruled. Backwoods Texas was another matter.

I watched him walk and followed him for a minute until he stopped to buy a beer. He looked at his watch. He was meeting someone, I surmised, otherwise time would not have meant anything to him.

I hung back and pretended to be waiting along with some husbands outside one of the small tents where vendors were selling locally made preserves and pickles to an excited cluster of women, all talking at once and sampling the wares.

About five long minutes passed, and then I saw Charlie's father. He went to shake hands with the boy, who rudely turned away and took a drink of his beer. He was above that kind of intimacy with a lowlife. Charlie appeared next, to his father's chagrin. I edged closer.

". . . told you to stay in the car," I picked up from his father's comment.

Charlie asked the boy his name. The boy gave Charlie's father a cold look. Charlie's father grabbed Charlie by the arm so hard I thought he'd break it, and forcefully sent him back in the direction from which he'd come.

The boy and Charlie's father exchanged words for a minute, Charlie's father nodded, and then they turned so they were almost headed in my direction.

I slipped quickly into the jams tent, watching them from behind some shelving. The proprietor asked me if I'd like to try some pickled garlic. I ignored her and followed the pair to the tent where I'd first seen the boy. Then the boy hung back and Charlie's father walked into the tent and approached the blonde whom the boy had harassed earlier. He smiled and shook hands with her. Her face lit up, and she nodded. She stood up and one of her friends did also, but Charlie's father motioned her to stay put. The blonde turned to her friend and I gathered she was conveying that she'd be back momentarily. Charlie's father led her out of the tent. Somehow, I'd lost track of the boy, but as Charlie's father walked by, he was close enough that I could hear him saying, "so we'd like a photo of all the raffle prize winners, you know, for the paper." The girl clapped her hands together, exclaiming, "I can't believe I won! Lord, I never win anything."

The situation was coming together in my mind. Charlie's father was the boy's fixer now that he was in Texas. The syndicate probably had bigger fish to fry, and they'd sublet the job, as they likely had done with other tasks in the past. Charlie's father was one of many small local gangs that assist larger regional crime organizations in much the way legitimate businesses operate. This was why so many mobsters sent their sons to college to get business degrees; the basic principles were all the same.

If the feds were coming in a few hours, that might be too late. The girl would be dead, or at least mortally wounded, by then. I cast about in my mind trying to figure out how to save her while following them at a distance in the crowd. My biggest problem was that I was alone. I'd have to derail the boy's plans somehow, while remaining unnoticed.

At that point, I remembered that I didn't have a car, so if they drove off, I couldn't follow them, but I reasoned I'd cross that bridge when I came to it. With so many problems facing me, I could only handle one at a time. I wished I'd finished a Zen course in maintaining presence that I'd abandoned a few years back. It would've come in handy.

As I walked, I gradually became aware that I was experiencing an odd mixture of hyper-alertness and fatigue. I felt like I was about to jump out of my skin at anything unexpected, yet my eyes felt like they were dead within the sockets, like I could've closed them and slept for days. Shock and exhaustion was a combination I'd never experienced; it was doubly uncomfortable particularly since it was unfamiliar.

Then I saw Charlie. He'd entered the stream of movement from the side and was headed in the same direction I was. I debated whether or not to try talking to him again. After making sure he was alone, I put my hand on his shoulder.

He turned quickly and was obviously startled to see me.

"You're alive!" he said.

"Yes, but they got Dylan," I told him.

"I need your help," he said.

"Where are they going?" I asked, indicating his father and the blonde.

"I think he's going to drive her somewhere out of town, but he has to tie her up first," he explained.

"Tie her up?" I said, "How the hell can he do that in this crowd?"

"There's a tent they have, that's where they're going," he said.

I had an idea.

"You keep an eye on her, I'll be right back," I said. I went into a tent selling items emblazoned with eagles, deer, and wild game. I've never stolen anything in my life, but I didn't have any money, so I pocketed a lighter with a flying goose on it while the vendor was busy wrapping up a large set of mounted antlers for a customer.

I ran to catch up with Charlie, who pointed at a small tent. Unlike all the others, it was completely obscured by tarps and zippers. It was meant to be some kind of private tent for musical performers, but Charlie's father had commandeered it for the boy. Inside, I could hear the sounds of a struggle and the high-pitched shrieking of the girl, which was swiftly muffled.

"Stand back," I said to Charlie as I set fire to an edge of the tent. It took a moment to get going, but once it did, it went up in a blaze of light.

Hollering came from inside the tent as Charlie's father and the boy scrambled to get out. I could see Charlie's father's face as he unzipped an opening near us, and then he was pushed out of the way by the boy, who came out looking furious.

We locked eyes and it was clear he knew I'd set the fire. Charlie's father came tumbling out after him, choking on the smoke that quickly filled the small tent.

Heedless of the boy's stare, I shouted to Charlie, "We've got to get her out of there!"

The two of us covered our faces with with the crooks of our arms and darted through a burned-out side of the tent, only to find the girl lying unconscious on the ground. They'd probably drugged her. Charlie swooped her up in his arms and ran back out of the tent. I emerged to see chaos everywhere—people screaming as the flames leapt higher and higher into the air and men raced to protect the adjacent tents, while others evacuated the crowds inside.

However, in the midst of the frantic melee, just one thing caught my attention: the face of the boy, still staring at me, his face lit by flames.

CHAPTER 19

Charlie's father was nowhere to be found, and after looking away to ascertain the girl's condition, I saw the boy had vanished.

Paramedics, who were already on site nearby in case there were any emergencies at the festival, raced over and began administering oxygen to her; I knew she'd be fine. "She's been drugged," I shouted, since they would think it strange in a few minutes when she didn't come out of what they would suppose was a faint. They looked at me quizzically, but Charlie grabbed my shoulder.

"We've got to go," he said urgently.

We started running; I was following Charlie, but it seemed he had no idea where he was going. Then he pointed to a small building and said, "Come on!"

Among the sea of festival tents was an unusual octagonal-shaped building with an equally odd octagonal steeple on top; it looked like a cross between a gazebo and a small misshapen barn. Charlie ran up to one of the walls, which actually turned out have a small a small door in it, jiggled the handle, and it opened. We climbed inside.

"I used to sneak in here when I was a teenager. It's the Vereins Kirche, one of the oldest buildings in town," he said.

Finally, Charlie's penchant for history had proven useful.

"Before you say anything," Charlie began, pausing to catch his breath, "I'm done with my father. It was a stupid thing to do, but like you said, I thought I could make him feel differently. Now I know he'll never change."

"I'm glad that realization is sending you in the right direction," I said. "Better late than never."

"Honestly, that's not what did it," he admitted.

"Huh?" I said.

"It was that kid," he explained. "I don't know how to say this, but I grew up knowing my father was into *all* kinds of stuff. Really bad stuff—pimping underage prostitutes, selling drugs to kids, you name it. It wasn't horrifying to me because it was just our life. I didn't know anything different." He paused, then continued, "This kid torturing women is something else."

At this point, Charlie must've seen a look of stupefaction on my face, because he said, "I know, to you it probably all seems the same, but when you're *in* it, you have—" he sought for a word, "*levels* of how bad different things are, and what that guy's doing is the worst, if that makes any sense," he added.

I tried to absorb what he'd said. It basically amounted to honor among thieves, or why murderers in prison killed child molesters. Evil had a hierarchy, just like virtue.

Whatever the reason, I was glad Charlie was out of that mess.

"Look," I told him, "There's a bunch of feds on their way down, they'll be here soon. They'll get your father, and I'll negotiate with them to get you off light. At least for most of this, you've assisted a federal agent, at risk to your own life—that should count for something."

“I didn’t know they were going to kill Dylan,” he said. “I’m sorry.”

I just shrugged. “He was a good man.” In my business, you couldn’t dwell on the unfairness of life or the vagaries of how things played out. You’d lose your mind.

“So are you,” Charlie offered. I looked up and I could see pain written across his face. It was a look of genuine contrition. I’d never seen it before, certainly never amongst the suspects I interrogated for unspeakable crimes, and I’ve never seen it since.

“If we could just find some evidence to link the kid to the murders,” I began.

“I’ve got the proof,” Charlie said. “They really did hire me to trace the kid’s DNA and it was linked to other branches of his family. It’s enough to convict.”

I was ecstatic. “You really are a genealogist?” I asked.

“Of course. That’s what I did after I left the bureau. I had to make a living, and I love research,” he said. “That’s what brought me to you.”

“To me?” I asked.

“Yeah. The hair clippings,” he explained.

I was perplexed. “What are you talking about?” I asked.

“All these years, I’ve been coming to you and stealing hair clippings when you weren’t looking. The salon is bugged and I booked my appointments right after you had mobsters in. Using hair for DNA isn’t ideal. I’d really need the follicles to get the best data, but it gave me enough to prove which crime families had been in the salon, and then I relayed what they’d told you about to my father. That’s how he was able to stay in the good graces of the syndicate he worked with. He had the best information in the business!” he said.

If I hadn’t already been sitting down, so help me, I would’ve fallen down. He’d just told me that my work as an undercover federal agent, which had been inviting the unwitting confessions of thugs, later resulted in their identities being confirmed with their hair-clippings using DNA analysis, and their plans were then broadcast to their rival organizations. In short, I’d gotten people to talk, and it was benefitting both the feds and the mobsters, thanks to Charlie, with his bugs and plastic bags.

I was speechless. I’d been conning the customers and Charlie’d been conning me.

Meanwhile, genealogy, the history of humanity played out in strands of hair, had surrounded me with a forest of family trees of whose existence I was completely oblivious.

“You know your face strongly resembles your great-great-grandfather’s,” he said, smiling and stating a name which—for obvious reasons—I can’t repeat here. “I managed to get some of your hair after you'd given yourself a trim one time. His portrait's in the London Museum. Very impressive."

My family may have had deep roots, but it felt like my life was unraveling by the second. If it weren't for those roots, I'd be whisked off the face of the earth with the next strong wind.

"It's okay," he said, noting my bewilderment. "You give good haircuts. Seriously."

"Thanks," I mumbled, slowly gathering my thoughts.

At last, I could see the whole picture. There was a sense of relief so palpable, I bit my lip to keep from crying. And Dylan—Dylan had died for this.

"There's something you should know," Charlie said, getting out his phone. "The other day when I started having my doubts about this, I made a list of all my father's associates and everyone I know in the syndicate. I also had some paperwork—bank deposits and that kind of thing." He typed something into his phone. "When I press this key," he continued, "It's all being sent to my contact at the bureau."

He pressed the key.

Now they had some information they might be able to use for convictions.

"And now for the most important part," he said.

"What do you mean?" I asked.

"The DNA information to convict that bastard," he said, typing.

A moment later, it was done.

I felt sure I could leverage Charlie's willingness to share incriminating information to get him a lighter sentence. Who knew? When he got out of prison, maybe we could be friends.

I thought of the scars on Charlie's back.

We were friends.

CHAPTER 20

It wasn't a long drive up to Balanced Rock, but it was dark and an unknown fear was growing within me.

Charlie said his father and the murderer were probably up at Balanced Rock, a local attraction consisting of a huge boulder naturally balanced on a tiny point, which had mysteriously come un-attached.

"Oughta call it 'Toppled Rock,' Pa says," joked Charlie.

I'd never seen Charlie in such a good mood, considering our grave task—we were going to locate the gang and hopefully by then, the feds would arrive and we could alert them, whereupon they'd make the arrests.

We were warned never to take a situation for granted, never to assume anything would be easy, even if it seemed like it would be. If something went sideways, we'd be unprepared to react. Maybe that's why I was nervous.

"I'm really done," Charlie said with satisfaction. "You know, I don't even care if I go to jail. At least I can look myself in the mirror. I may be fat and stupid, but I'm not a criminal."

"You're not fat and stupid," I said. "Okay," I admitted, "You could stand to drop a few pounds, but who couldn't? Nobody's perfect."

"This probably sounds strange to you, since you're still in, but right now, I feel the way I did when I was on my first assignments, before I realized I wasn't any good at being a fed. I mean, I feel good about what we're doing," he said.

"You should. We're capturing a vicious killer and bringing him to justice," I said, adding, "In fact, we couldn't do this without you. Your evidence is what's going to hang him."

We approached the parking area off the road and sure enough, there were several of the cars belonging to the members of Charlie's father's gang.

"Where are they?" I asked, looking around.

"Up there," he said, pointing to the top of the mountain.

"What?!" I exclaimed. "I can't climb up there."

"You can. Even I can do it," he said. "It's not that hard. There's a path."

Owing to years of having climbed to the top in his youth, Charlie led the way confidently, even as we walked through the dark.

About a third of the way up, observing me grabbing a rock to steady myself as I hiked up a steep part, Charlie warned, "Don't put your hands under the rocks. That's where the rattlers' nests are." He needn't have feared I'd do it again. I kept my hands to myself the rest of the walk.

We stopped a little further on, mainly so Charlie could catch his breath.

"I'm really thinking of getting into shape," he said quietly. "Maybe get myself a girlfriend."

"That blonde at the festival would probably be grateful if she knew you'd saved her. You rescued her like a pro," I whispered. Charlie beamed so effusively I could actually see his smile in the dark.

We continued on until we got near the top. Charlie's father, the gang, and the murderer were sitting around a small campfire. We eavesdropped for a minute. Apparently, they were hiding out on top of the mountain so they could get a vantage point on any cops or feds headed out to the ranch, where they'd obviously be expected to be holed up. Being out in the open, they increased their chances for escape. The boy was taking a private plane back east early in the morning and they were just killing a bit of time so he wouldn't have to spend much time at the airport and be noticed or hassled by authorities. Airports were definitely the least anonymous place on earth to be.

I figured he'd found Texas to be a poor hunting ground and missed being in a place where his name meant something. It was a foolish move, though, as his circle in New England had begun to turn on him, but psychopaths generally make stupid decisions because they overestimate their ability to control everything.

Charlie motioned for me to come down the mountain a bit, and he texted his contact that everyone was on the mountain. If they could surround them, they'd have them. I worried about the light from the screen attracting attention but didn't see anyone. Then I heard a click that made my stomach drop—the sound of a gun being cocked.

"Get going," said a gravelly voice, and we were forced back up the mountain. I didn't want to try anything cute because it was too dark to see and someone could get shot. Besides, the feds would be there any minute.

Once at the top, the sight of the boy's face, lit again, as it was, by firelight, seemed somehow appropriate. He glared when he saw me. I stopped in my tracks.

"Pa, it's over," Charlie said, approaching his father. "The feds are coming for you. I tipped them off."

Charlie's father registered no surprise. "Now ain't that somethin'," he said blandly. Then he stood up to his full height, slowly came to Charlie, and grabbed him by the arm. I saw Charlie wince in pain. The old man hurtled Charlie towards the kid, who was suddenly holding a gun.

It was as if they'd forgotten I existed, so consumed were they in meting out their own version of justice to Charlie, who'd betrayed them. I suppose they felt I was just doing my job, but Charlie had committed treason of the highest order—he'd squealed on family.

The kid reached into a backpack and pulled out what looked like an orange flotation device of some kind. Handing it to Charlie, he commanded, "Put this on." Charlie wrapped it around his waist and the kid said, "Buckle it." Just then, seeing the wires, I realized what it was, but before I could shout out to him, the buckle was secured, a light went on, and Charlie was a human bomb.

The kid held the detonator. "This guy's my ticket out of here," he said, adding, as he glanced in my direction, "So that just leaves you."

“I’m a federal agent,” I said. “My backup is on their way. If you kill me, they’ll get you.”

“I don’t think so,” he said calmly. “My father’ll see to that.”

“There’s a limit to what you can do,” I said, my voice getting louder. I’d heard the rustle of some brush behind me and wanted to cover the sound of the feds approaching. I also wanted to let them know what was in progress. “You think you’re in control because you’ve got my friend in a bomb belt and you’ve got me at gunpoint, but to me, it looks like you’ve got your hands full.”

What happened next was so unexpected, so shocking, I can hardly even bear to recall it, but I’ll try.

As the federal agents swarmed around us, calling out, “Hands up!” the kid raised his gun to fire at me. Charlie knocked the gun out of the kid’s hand and clasped both of his hands around the detonator.

Then he pressed the button.

The explosion sent me flying about five feet, and the only thing that stopped me was a large rock that I practically splattered against. A few members of Charlie’s father’s gang were lying on the ground, burned and missing limbs. They were screaming. Charlie’s father was gone. The kid was gone.

Charlie was gone.

It felt like forever until I inhaled, and when I did, I felt a flood of hot tears pouring down my face. I shivered in the cold night air, looking around at the feds; they were okay, they’d just been thrown back by the explosion like I’d been. Only those closest to the center had perished.

Someone helped me down the mountain, I don’t remember who, and there was an ambulance, and I have a vague memory of being rolled into a hospital on a stretcher. A doctor leaned over me saying, “You’ll be okay.” She smiled.

CHAPTER 21

Everyone has secrets.

They hold them tightly. I should know, because I was unsuccessful at obtaining them until I posed as someone who wasn’t trying to get them at all.

So that’s what happened.

And about Charlie? Charlie had every reason in the world to be crooked. It would’ve been the easiest thing to do. I understood how it was with him, that when your family needs you to be a certain thing and you can’t or won’t, they’ll turn on you in a second.

Despite all this—all the years of indoctrination into crime—in the end, Charlie still chose to be a better person.

That's the amazing thing about good: it can come out of anywhere. It manifests spontaneously. Someone raised with brutality, greed, or hate can become the opposite, and for no discernable reason. Yes, good can come out of anywhere, but evil always has a pedigree.

There's just one more thing I'd like to tell you. It's a special secret.

There's a unique monument in Washington, D.C., somewhere right out in plain sight. I can't tell you where it is, but it bears the initials of certain deceased members of the bureau, men and women who died saving others. Hundreds of people walk right past it every day without even being aware of what it is. Nobody can ever know their names or what they did, except those of us who worked with them. And we can never tell.

I know the names of several people whose bravery is honored there, and now Charlie's is one of them.

If you ever visit Washington, you'll probably pass right by and never know.

As for me, I'll never forget.

About the Author

Born in Manhattan and raised in Texas, Cinzi Lavin is the award-winning creator of several full-length original musical dramas, novels, and numerous theatrical works. With professional experience as an actress, singer, instrumentalist, and educator, her career highlights include a performance by invitation at the White House. In addition to receiving state and national honors for her influence on American culture, she is a fellow of the Royal Society of Arts. She and her husband make their home in Litchfield County, Connecticut.

Other Titles by Cinzi Lavin

□

The Taciturn Sky

An inheritance changes Bryce Parnell's world in ways he never imagined. As a traitor to his class, he struggles to find his place somewhere between his Old Money upbringing and the uncultivated world he has come to know. Dividing his time between Larchmont, New York and Norfolk, Connecticut, he inexpertly navigates romantic relationships and interacts uneasily with wealthy friends and family, all the while hoping to outrun a reality of which he is becoming increasingly aware: that he is witnessing the last days of genteel aristocracy. Set amidst a backdrop of exclusive events and elite gatherings, Bryce savors treasured memories of his privileged past, yet slowly begins forging new paradigms of nobility.

Nemesis of the Great

In this sequel to *The Taciturn Sky*, Bryce Parnell is forced to reconsider his position as a member of the elite class once he discovers who is actually running things from above. Set in the twilight of America's genteel aristocracy, he comes to terms with the fact that he and his kind are an endangered species, about to be overtaken by the rise of the newly rich and their limitless money and power. An unintentional spiritual odyssey, an unexpected friendship, and a heartbreaking family tragedy are only part of his new world, as Bryce ultimately accepts that in order to outrun his enemies, he will have to run faster than he has ever run in his life.

www.ingramcontent.com/pod-product-compliance
Lightning Source LLC
LaVergne TN
LVHW050940080826
845145LV00004B/1340

* 9 7 8 1 7 3 6 6 3 5 0 2 5 *